THE
LAND
OF
STORIES

THE ULTIMATE
BOOK HUGGER'S
GUIDE

Praise for the Land of Stories Series

"A **magical** debut." —*Family Circle*

"**Captivating.**" —*Teen Vogue*

"In *The Land of Stories*, Colfer showcases his talent
for crafting **fancifully imaginative** plots
and multidimensional characters."
—*Los Angeles Times*

"There's **more** in Colfer's **magic kingdoms**
than Disney has dreamt of."
—*USA Today*

"It will hit big with its combination of
earnestness and playful poise."
—*The New York Times Book Review*

"It's hard not to love [the book]....the nifty ending ties
the plot's multiple strands up while leaving room for
further **fairy tale adventures**."
—*Publishers Weekly*

THE LAND OF STORIES

THE ULTIMATE BOOK HUGGER'S GUIDE

CHRIS COLFER

ILLUSTRATED BY
BRANDON DORMAN

LITTLE, BROWN AND COMPANY
NEW YORK BOSTON

Copyright © 2018 by Christopher Colfer
Excerpt from *A Tale of Magic...* copyright © 2019 by Christopher Colfer
Illustrations copyright © 2018 by Brandon Dorman

Cover art copyright © 2018 by Brandon Dorman
Cover design by Sasha Illingworth
Cover copyright © 2018 by Hachette Book Group, Inc.

Little, Brown and Company
Hachette Book Group
1290 Avenue of the Americas, New York, NY 10104
Visit us at LBYR.com

Originally published in hardcover and ebook
by Little, Brown and Company in October 2018
First Trade Paperback Edition: August 2020

Little, Brown and Company is a division of Hachette Book Group, Inc.
The Little, Brown name and logo are trademarks of Hachette Book Group, Inc.

The publisher is not responsible for websites (or their content) that
are not owned by the publisher.

The Library of Congress has cataloged the hardcover edition as follows:
Names: Colfer, Chris, 1990– author. | Dorman, Brandon, illustrator.
Title: The Land of Stories : the ultimate book hugger's guide / Chris Colfer ;
illustrated by Brandon Dorman.
Description: First edition. | New York : Little, Brown and Company, 2018. |
Audience: Age 8–12.
Identifiers: LCCN 2018009915| ISBN 9780316523301 (hardcover) |
ISBN 9780316419918 (large-print hardcover) | ISBN 9780316523318 (ebook) |
ISBN 9780316523332 (library ebook edition)
Subjects: LCSH: Colfer, Chris, 1990– Land of Stories—Miscellanea. | Colfer, Chris,
1990– Land of Stories—Juvenile literature.
Classification: LCC PS3603.O4369 Z76 2018 | DDC 813/.6—dc23
LC record available at https://lccn.loc.gov/2018009915

ISBNs: 978-0-316-52343-1 (pbk.), 978-0-316-52331-8 (ebook)

Printed in China

APS

10 9 8 7 6 5 4 3 2 1

To Heather,
for guiding my reality so I can
live in a fairy-tale world.
This one's for you!

CONTENTS

INTRODUCTION

Hello, readers from around the globe, and welcome to *The Land of Stories: The Ultimate Book Hugger's Guide*!

Whether you're new to the Land of Stories series or you've read each book a dozen times, this guide will tell you everything you'll need to know to become an official Book Hugger.

We'll review everything about Alex and Conner Bailey, their colorful friends and family, the magical creatures they encounter, the enchanted places they explore, and all the evildoers they overcome.

Warning—this guide may contain some spoilers of the Bailey twins' adventures through the fairy-tale world and beyond. So if you like to be surprised, please put this book in a safe place until you're ready.

Otherwise, sit back, relax, and enjoy your journey through the Land of Stories!

WHO'S WHO

in the

LAND

of

STORIES

HEROES

ALEX BAILEY

lex is a young woman who is wise beyond her years. As a child, she had a thirst for knowledge and read every book she could get her hands on. Unfortunately, Alex was often teased at school for her intelligence, and it was difficult for her to make friends. She spent the majority of her early days feeling misunderstood and lonely.

However, all that changes during her adventures in the Land of Stories. Thanks to Alex's cleverness, she and her brother, Conner, are able to save the fairy-tale world on many different occasions. Her wisdom is celebrated, and she grows from an underappreciated teacher's pet to a confident world leader.

SPECIES: Human/fairy
BIRTHPLACE: The Otherworld
OCCUPATION: Student/leader of the Happily Forever After Assembly
TRADEMARK: Intelligence
NEVER WITHOUT: A plan

Conner is a creative and funny young man—and although he wouldn't admit it, he has a very big heart. During his childhood, Conner struggled in school. He thought the classroom was a great place to take naps and practice new jokes, but he never thought it would help him put his imagination to good use.

After some encouragement from his teacher, Mrs. Peters, Conner begins writing short stories and discovers he has a knack for storytelling—and luckily, he discovers it just in time! Thanks to his imaginative writing, Conner and his sister are able to recruit an army of his characters and save both worlds from a sinister plot.

SPECIES: Human/fairy
BIRTHPLACE: The Otherworld
OCCUPATION: Student/future author
TRADEMARK: Imagination
NEVER WITHOUT: A joke

THE FAIRY GODMOTHER

The Fairy Godmother is the Bailey twins' grandmother and the leader of the fairy-tale world. She is known for her compassionate heart and powerful magic—everything from granting poor maidens' wishes, to slaying fire-breathing dragons. The Fairy Godmother is the founder of the Happily Ever After Assembly, which peacefully unites the leaders of all the kingdoms and territories.

The Fairy Godmother was the first person from the Land of Stories to discover our world, and she named it the Otherworld. When she first arrived, the Otherworld was in a dark period of war and famine. By spreading the stories of the fairy-tale world into ours, she and the other fairies inspired several generations to be brave, to believe in themselves, and to be kind to one another, and introduced them to the joys of a "happily ever after."

SPECIES: Fairy
BIRTHPLACE: The Charming Kingdom
OCCUPATION: Leader of the Happily
Ever After Assembly
TRADEMARK: Compassion
NEVER WITHOUT: A wand

PRINCE CHARLIE "FROGGY" CHARMING

Froggy is the youngest prince in the Charming Dynasty and was cursed to look like a frog when he was a young man. Fearing that his family would never accept him, Froggy ran into the forest and lived in hiding for many years. It's in the forest that Froggy first meets the Bailey twins, and if it wasn't for his kindness, Alex and Conner would have never found their way home.

The Bailey twins become Froggy's closest friends, and he is always eager to join their various quests to save the fairy-tale world. During their very first escapade, Froggy meets the future love of his life, Queen Red Riding Hood. After Queen Red loses her throne, the people of her kingdom elect Froggy as their new king. Even though Froggy has the opportunity to change back into a human, he decides his amphibian form suits him best.

SPECIES: Human turned amphibian
BIRTHPLACE: The Charming Kingdom
OCCUPATION: Recluse/king
TRADEMARK: Helpfulness
NEVER WITHOUT: Lily pad tea

QUEEN RED RIDING HOOD

People's first impression of Queen Red Riding Hood is that she's a selfish, misguided, materialistic, and naïve young woman—and she *is*—but beneath all the diamond necklaces is a heart of gold. She always means well but rarely knows what she means.

After her childhood encounter with the Big Bad Wolf, Red was elected queen of her own kingdom. She lived an extravagant and pampered lifestyle until meeting the Bailey twins—then Red is thrown into one life-threatening situation after another. But with every passing obstacle, more of Red's selflessness, sensibility, and compassion shine through—or at least, that's what she thinks.

SPECIES: Human
BIRTHPLACE: The Center Kingdom (formerly part of the Northern Kingdom)
OCCUPATION: Queen
TRADEMARK: Misguidedness
NEVER WITHOUT: A tiara

GOLDILOCKS

Goldilocks is a strong and willful woman with unlimited courage. There is no opponent she can't outsmart or outfight—which comes in handy during her adventures with the Bailey twins.

After her scandal with the Three Bears, Goldilocks was labeled a young vandal in her village. She ran away from home and has been a wanted fugitive ever since. However, we soon learn that Goldilocks was tricked into going to the home of the Three Bears and that her story isn't what it seems.

SPECIES: Human
BIRTHPLACE: The Center Kingdom
(formerly part of the Northern Kingdom)
OCCUPATION: Thief/vigilante
TRADEMARK: Courage
NEVER WITHOUT: A sword

JACK

After climbing a beanstalk and slaying a giant, Jack became famous throughout the kingdoms for his bravery. However, the bravest act of his life wasn't slaying a giant, but following his heart. Jack decides to give up his heroic reputation and the chance to be Queen Red Riding Hood's king to be with the woman he loves.

Jack and Goldilocks enjoy a life on the run and come out of hiding only when the twins need their help.

Eventually, Jack and Goldilocks are married and start a family. Their first child is a boy whom they strategically name Hero so that their son will always be the *hero* of his own story.

SPECIES: Human
BIRTHPLACE: The Center Kingdom (formerly part of the Northern Kingdom)
OCCUPATION: Hero/vigilante
TRADEMARK: Bravery
NEVER WITHOUT: An axe

MOTHER GOOSE

Mother Goose is a sassy, flask-sipping, sharp-tongued old lady who's infamous for starting trouble in every dimension she enters. While helping the Fairy Godmother spread fairy tales in the Otherworld, Mother Goose rubbed elbows with everyone from Leonardo da Vinci to Walt Disney. It's even rumored that Mother Goose started the Italian Renaissance after throwing a killer party in Florence.

Despite all the drama she causes, Mother Goose knows how to have a good time. She teaches the Bailey twins that no matter how dangerous a situation may be, you can always walk away with a good story.

MOTHER GOOSE:
SPECIES: Nonspecific
BIRTHPLACE: Secretive
OCCUPATION: Nobody really knows
TRADEMARK: Inappropriateness
NEVER WITHOUT: A flask

LESTER:
SPECIES: Gander
BIRTHPLACE: Mother Goose's cabin
OCCUPATION: Transportation services/confidant
TRADEMARK: Judgment
NEVER WITHOUT: Opinions

LESTER

Lester is a horse-sized gander and Mother Goose's companion. She won his egg in a card game, and once he hatched and grew to his enormous size, he became her favorite mode of transportation. Sometimes when Mother Goose is away, Lester likes to dress up in her bonnets and fly around—which is why many people in the Otherworld believe Mother Goose is an overgrown goose herself.

TROLLBELLA

Trollbella has the mind of a ruthless dictator but the heart of a lovesick teenager—a very dangerous combination. After large rocks mysteriously fall on the Troll and Goblin Kings, Trollbella inherits the throne of their underground territory. She's determined to bring class back to the troll and goblin species and forces her people to bathe and spend hours each day learning rigorous dance routines.

Trollbella has been in love with Conner since the moment she laid eyes on him. She lovingly refers to him as her Butterboy—which sends shivers down his spine every time she says it.

SPECIES: Troll
BIRTHPLACE: The Troll and Goblin Territory
OCCUPATION: Queen
TRADEMARK: Lust
NEVER WITHOUT: Butterboy

JOHN BAILEY

John Bailey was Alex and Conner's father and the Fairy Godmother's son. He was very passionate about fairy tales and raised the twins on the lessons and morals that the stories teach. Although it's kept a complete secret from the twins at first, John was born and raised in the Land of Stories. It was always his dream to take his children to his home one day; unfortunately, he never got the chance. John passed away shortly before the twins' eleventh birthday.

During their first visit to the fairy-tale world, the twins follow a journal that helps them collect items for the legendary Wishing Spell. Eventually they learn that their father wrote the journal, and therefore they get to experience the Land of Stories with him after all.

SPECIES: Human/fairy
BIRTHPLACE: The Fairy Kingdom
OCCUPATION: Father/storyteller
TRADEMARK: Adventure
NEVER WITHOUT: A good story

CHARLOTTE BAILEY

Charlotte is Alex and Conner's mom and a nurse at the local children's hospital. She is a wonderful and courageous mother and would do anything for her children. She works tirelessly to support her family following her husband's death, but eventually she finds love again and marries Dr. Bob Gordon.

Sometimes hearing about her children's magical adventures can be a little much for Charlotte, so the twins have to abbreviate the details to prevent her from panicking. Having such a capable son and daughter fills Charlotte with pride, but she enjoys it when they still need her from time to time.

SPECIES: Human
BIRTHPLACE: The Otherworld
OCCUPATION: Nurse
TRADEMARK: Concern
NEVER WITHOUT: Nursing scrubs

DR. BOB GORDON

r. Bob Gordon is Alex and Conner's caring stepfather. He's a surgeon at the children's hospital where Charlotte works. Having lost a spouse himself, Bob has a lot in common with Charlotte, and they comfort each other through their grief. Eventually that comfort turns into romance, and the two become engaged.

At first the twins aren't sure how they feel about their mother remarrying, but time after time, Bob proves his devotion to his family by risking his life to protect them. Joining a new family is always a difficult task—especially a magical family—but Bob has never complained and is always there when the twins need him.

SPECIES: Human
BIRTHPLACE: The Otherworld
OCCUPATION: Surgeon
TRADEMARK: Adaptability
NEVER WITHOUT: A stethoscope

BREE CAMPBELL

Bree is Conner's classmate and his first crush. She enjoys reading mystery novels and likes to write her own short stories, too. When Conner goes on an excursion across Europe to save the fairy-tale world, Bree volunteers to accompany him and proves to be the perfect companion. After visiting the Land of Stories and learning that Conner's family comes from magic blood, Bree begins asking questions about her own family. She discovers there's magic in her family's blood, too, and that they're part of a centuries-old secret society known as the Sisters Grimm.

SPECIES: Human
BIRTHPLACE: The Otherworld
OCCUPATION: Student/writer/future US senator
TRADEMARK: Problem solving
NEVER WITHOUT: Headphones

EMMERICH HIMMELSBACH

Emmerich is a German boy Conner and Bree meet by chance. He helps them sneak into Neuschwanstein Castle and access a secret portal that leads into the fairy-tale world. Over time, Emmerich learns that his encounter with Conner and Bree wasn't as accidental as it appeared. He discovers he's the secret son of the Masked Man and Bo Peep and that his mother took him to Germany to protect him from his father. Later, Emmerich is kidnapped by witches and used in a gruesome plot to control his father and the army of literary villains that the Masked Man is recruiting.

SPECIES: Human
BIRTHPLACE: The Center Kingdom (formerly known as the Red Riding Hood Kingdom)
OCCUPATION: Curious child
TRADEMARK: Curiosity
NEVER WITHOUT: A question

MRS. PETERS

Mrs. Peters is the Bailey twins' sixth-grade teacher, who later becomes their principal. In the beginning, Mrs. Peters and Conner don't get along and she constantly sends him to detention for misbehaving in class. As time goes on, though, Mrs. Peters discovers Conner's writing talent and encourages him to develop it. Shortly after retiring, Mrs. Peters confesses that Conner is her favorite student—not because he got the best grades, but because of the *progress* he made over the years.

SPECIES: Human
BIRTHPLACE: The Otherworld
OCCUPATION: Teacher/principal
TRADEMARK: Encouragement
NEVER WITHOUT: A detention slip

ROOK ROBINS

Rook lives on a farm with his father, Farmer Robins, in the Eastern Kingdom. He becomes friends with Alex while she's training to become the Fairy Godmother's apprentice. The two become very close, and Rook is Alex's first kiss.

Alex makes the mistake of trusting Rook with a big secret, and unfortunately, he betrays her in order to save his father. Rook spends the rest of his life trying to make it up to her.

SPECIES: Human
BIRTHPLACE: The Eastern Kingdom
OCCUPATION: Farmer's son
TRADEMARK: Devotion
NEVER WITHOUT: An apology

HAGETTA

Hagetta is a witch who lives in the Dwarf Forests. Although she comes from a family of witches who practice the dark arts, Hagetta uses only white magic. She heals people with the flames of an albino dragon that she keeps burning in her fireplace at all times. When Goldilocks was a girl and ran away from her village, Hagetta looked after her and gave Goldilocks her very first sword. She taught her a valuable lesson that Goldilocks later passed along to the Bailey twins: "Courage is one thing no one can ever take from you."

SPECIES: Witch
BIRTHPLACE: The Dwarf Forests
OCCUPATION: Mistress of white magic
TRADEMARK: Warmth
NEVER WITHOUT: The healing flames of an albino dragon

PORRIDGE, BUCKLE, AND OATS

Porridge, Buckle, and Oats are the family of horses that help the Bailey twins and their friends on their journeys across the fairy-tale world. Porridge is the fastest horse in all the kingdoms and has been Goldilocks's faithful steed for many years. She later meets Buckle, an obnoxious stallion, in the stables of Queen Red Riding Hood's castle. Porridge and Buckle have a son who is named Oats after his multicolored hide.

SPECIES: Horse
BIRTHPLACE: Various
OCCUPATION: Noble steeds/confidants
TRADEMARK: Loyalty
NEVER WITHOUT: Their masters

CORNELIUS

Cornelius is a frumpy unicorn with a broken horn. Despite all the beautiful unicorns in his herd, Alex selects Cornelius to help her with her fairy duties because Cornelius has the best heart. Like all unicorns, Cornelius can run ten times faster than any horse. His horn acts as a magical locating device so he can take his rider to wherever or whatever they need.

SPECIES: Unicorn
BIRTHPLACE: The Fairy Kingdom
OCCUPATION: Magical steed/confidant
TRADEMARK: Lovability
NEVER WITHOUT: Direction

CLAWDIUS

Clawdius is a black wolf and Red Riding Hood's pet. Mistaken for a dog, Clawdius is rescued by Red from the cold mountains of the Northern Kingdom when he is just a pup. She names him Clawdius after a character in William Shakespeare's *Hamlet*—or as Red likes to call it, William Shakeyfruit's *Hamhead*. By the time Clawdius's true species is revealed, Red loves him too much to give him up. Thanks to him, Red overcomes her fear of wolves.

SPECIES: Wolf
BIRTHPLACE: The Northern Kingdom
OCCUPATION: Royal pet
TRADEMARK: Appetite
NEVER WITHOUT: A treat

RED RIDING HOOD'S GRANNY

Red Riding Hood's granny is a very sweet and gentle old woman. A former revolutionist, Granny serves as Queen Red's top advisor when she's elected to the throne. Thanks to her impeccable sewing skills, Granny is able to stitch all of Red's old ball gowns into a balloon for a flying ship that Red and her friends travel in during their mission to defeat Ezmia, the evil Enchantress. Once construction is complete, Queen Red christens the ship the *Granny* in her granny's honor.

SPECIES: Human
BIRTHPLACE: The Center Kingdom
(formerly part of the Northern Kingdom)
OCCUPATION: Royal advisor/seamstress
TRADEMARK: Hospitality
NEVER WITHOUT: Knitting needles

BO PEEP

Little Bo Peep is a shepherdess and owner of the Bo Peep Family Farms. She challenges Queen Red Riding Hood's throne and is elected queen after defeating Red in a fiery debate. At first, Bo Peep's intentions seem entirely selfless, but Bo Peep is using the throne to hide a heartbreaking secret she's kept quiet for years.

SPECIES: Human
BIRTHPLACE: The Center Kingdom
(formerly part of the Northern Kingdom)
OCCUPATION: Landowner/queen
TRADEMARK: Secrets
NEVER WITHOUT: A heart locket

THE FAIRY COUNCIL

The Fairy Council is in charge of the Fairy Kingdom and oversees the Happily Forever After Assembly. It consists of Rosette, Tangerina, Xathous, Emerelda, Skylene, Violetta, and Coral. They each embody a color of the rainbow and a specific set of tasks. Although they

do their best to maintain order throughout the kingdoms, the Fairy Council is very old-fashioned and often bumps heads with the Bailey twins.

SPECIES: Fairy
BIRTHPLACE: Various
OCCUPATION: Members of the Happily Ever After Assembly/Happily Forever After Assembly
TRADEMARK: Color
NEVER WITHOUT: Old-fashioned values

THE HAPPILY FOREVER AFTER ASSEMBLY

When Alex becomes the Fairy Godmother, the Happily Ever After Assembly is renamed the Happily Forever After Assembly to be more inclusive. The current members include the Fairy Council, King Chance Charming and Queen Cinderella, King Froggy and Queen Red Riding Hood, Queen Snow White and King Chandler Charming, Queen Sleeping Beauty and King Chase Charming, Queen Rapunzel and Sir William,

Queen Trollbella, and Empress Elvina. The assembly doesn't always agree, but each member is devoted to keeping peace between the nations.

SPECIES: Human, fairy, troll, goblin, elf
BIRTHPLACE: Various
OCCUPATION: Kingdom and territory leaders/representatives
TRADEMARK: Diplomacy
NEVER WITHOUT: Hope

THE SISTERS GRIMM

The Sisters Grimm are the descendants of the Brothers Grimm and are a secret society that tracks magical happenings throughout the Otherworld. They're the first people to discover an approaching collision between the fairy-tale world and the Otherworld that will result in a permanent gateway. Cornelia Grimm administrates the society with the help of her daughter, Frenda, and her niece, Wanda.

SPECIES: Human
BIRTHPLACE: The Otherworld
OCCUPATION: Secret society
TRADEMARK: Observation
NEVER WITHOUT: Tools

THE BOOK HUGGERS

The Book Huggers are a reading club at Alex and Conner's school. The members include Mindy, Cindy, Lindy, and Wendy, who have been best friends since the first grade. After the Bailey twins exhibit some suspicious behavior at school, the Book Huggers decide to get to the bottom of what is going on. Over the course of an exhausting and obsessive search for the truth, the Book Huggers make the greatest discovery of their young lives.

SPECIES: Human
BIRTHPLACE: The Otherworld
OCCUPATION: Conspiracists
TRADEMARK: Suspicion
NEVER WITHOUT: Evidence

VILLAINS

THE EVIL QUEEN

The Evil Queen is Snow White's wicked stepmother. Although many are familiar with the story of Snow White, very few know about the Evil Queen's life beforehand. Her name was Evly and she was kidnapped as a child and forced to work as a slave for Ezmia, the evil Enchantress. When the love of Evly's life tried to rescue her, the Enchantress imprisoned him inside her Magic Mirror. Evly was so heartbroken, she paid a witch to cut out her heart and turn it into stone so she wouldn't feel the pain.

With the help of her faithful Huntsman and Huntress, the Evil Queen uses the legendary Wishing Spell to free the man trapped inside her Magic Mirror. Sadly, the man had been trapped inside the mirror for too long, and he dies in the Evil Queen's arms. During an attack on her castle, the Magic Mirror falls on top of the Evil Queen and she disappears inside it.

SPECIES: Human
BIRTHPLACE: Unknown
OCCUPATION: Former queen of the Northern Kingdom/wanted fugitive
TRADEMARK: Determination
NEVER WITHOUT: A heart of stone

MALUMCLAW

Malumclaw is the son of the Big Bad Wolf, who attacked Red Riding Hood as a child. After the death of his father, Malumclaw founded the Big Bad Wolf Pack with the other wolves to avenge their slain family members. Their reign of terror on farming communities is what inspired villagers to separate from the Northern Kingdom and form their own government and surround their country with a protective wall to keep the wolves at bay.

SPECIES: Wolf
BIRTHPLACE: Unknown
OCCUPATION: Predator
TRADEMARK: Grudges
NEVER WITHOUT: A pack

EZMIA THE ENCHANTRESS

Ezmia is the most powerful and vengeful threat the Bailey twins face. The Fairy Godmother found Ezmia in the Otherworld and brought her to the Fairy Kingdom to teach her magic. Ezmia quickly surpassed all the other fairies and became the Fairy Godmother's first apprentice. Although the honor was well deserved, all the other fairies became jealous, and they ostracized Ezmia.

After a series of heartbreaks, and with no friends to comfort her, Ezmia snapped and became the evil Enchantress. She imprisoned all the souls of the men who had broken her heart in jars and placed them on her mantel. Ezmia committed some of the greatest crimes in the fairy-tale world, most notably cursing Sleeping Beauty with the spinning wheel.

Eventually, Ezmia attempts to expand her reign of terror into the Otherworld. By dominating the fairy-tale world's past, present, and future and mastering the seven deadly sins, the Enchantress manifests a portal between worlds. Luckily, the Bailey twins stop her with the mythical Wand of Wonderment.

SPECIES: Fairy
BIRTHPLACE: The Otherworld
OCCUPATION: Former member of the Happily Ever After Assembly
TRADEMARK: Vengeance
NEVER WITHOUT: Jars of souls

RUMPELSTILTSKIN

Rumpelstiltskin is the youngest brother of the Seven Dwarves. Unlike the rest of his family, Rumpelstiltskin didn't want to spend his life working in the dwarf mines and began pursuing other interests. The Enchantress taught him magic, and he became her apprentice, but shortly after joining her, Rumpelstiltskin knew she was up to no good. Rumpelstiltskin turned himself in to Pinocchio Prison for his association with her crimes—but it doesn't take Ezmia long to track him down.

SPECIES: Dwarf
BIRTHPLACE: The Dwarf Forests
OCCUPATION: Former miner/
magical apprentice
TRADEMARK: Guilt
NEVER WITHOUT: A flower

THE SNOW QUEEN

The Snow Queen is a weather witch who lives in seclusion in the Northern Mountains. She once had power over the Northern Kingdom, until the House of White and their army chased her out. Losing her throne made her so distraught, she cried until her eyes froze and then melted away. Now she wears a cloth over her empty eye sockets.

The Snow Queen is often accompanied by two large polar bears that act as her servants and also pull her sleigh when she travels. She has possession of the last existing dragon egg and keeps it frozen at the bottom of an icy lake. Eventually, the Snow Queen forms a plan for the witches to leave the fairy-tale dimension and take over the Otherworld.

SPECIES: Witch
BIRTHPLACE: Unknown
OCCUPATION: Mistress of dark magic/
weather witch
TRADEMARK: Coldness
NEVER WITHOUT: An ice scepter

THE SEA WITCH

The Sea Witch is most famous for transforming the Little Mermaid's tail into legs. She lives in an underwater canyon deep below the surface of the ocean. She makes a living by trading magical favors with merpeople and sea creatures—but if they fail to pay her back, she imprisons them for eternity.

The Sea Witch has a pet cuttlefish and a school of great white sharks to do her bidding. She helps the Snow Queen create a plan to take over the Otherworld, and when a gateway between worlds appears, she leads the witches through it.

SPECIES: Merperson/witch
BIRTHPLACE: Mermaid Bay
OCCUPATION: Mistress of dark magic/tradeswoman
TRADEMARK: Negotiation
NEVER WITHOUT: Salt water

GENERAL
JACQUES DU MARQUIS

Jacques du Marquis was a general in Napoleon's Grande Armée in the early nineteenth century. He showed a great interest in the tales of the Brothers Grimm and had them followed by his soldiers. When the general learned the fairy-tale world was real, he led a battalion through a portal with plans of conquering the Land of Stories in the name of France. Having been outshone by Napoleon his entire military career, the general was certain the seizure of another dimension would put him back on top.

Unfortunately, the portal they traveled into had been tampered with. The general and his men were trapped between worlds for more than two hundred years. When they finally arrive, the general and the Grande Armée are a destructive force unlike anything the fairy-tale world has ever seen.

SPECIES: Human
BIRTHPLACE: The Otherworld
OCCUPATION: General of Napoleon's Grand Armée
TRADEMARK: Ruthlessness
NEVER WITHOUT: A map

THE MASKED MAN

The Masked Man is a mysterious prisoner who General Marquis frees from Pinocchio Prison to assist him in conquering the Land of Stories. He helps the general track down a dragon egg and raises the dragon into a ferocious fire-breathing monster. Unfortunately for the general and his men, the Masked Man uses the dragon against them.

When the dragon is defeated, the Masked Man breaks into the Fairy Palace and steals the Portal Potion from the Fairy Godmother's collection. Using the potion, the Masked Man travels into worlds of classic literature and recruits an army of literary villains to secure his own takeover. Eventually, the Bailey twins discover that the Masked Man is their evil uncle Lloyd, whom the Fairy Godmother had sent to Pinocchio Prison with a mask to hide his identity.

SPECIES: Human
BIRTHPLACE: The Fairy Kingdom
OCCUPATION: Scoundrel
TRADEMARK: Deception
NEVER WITHOUT: Stolen goods

MORINA

Morina isn't the strongest foe the Bailey twins face, but she's the most intelligent, and that makes her the most dangerous of all. She makes beauty potions by kidnapping children and bottling their life force. Being part troll, Morina was very unattractive growing up and created the potions for herself before selling them.

When she was younger, Morina cursed Prince Charlie Charming to look like a frog after he ended their brief romance. She later inserts herself into the witches' plan to take over the Otherworld but betrays them when she gives the same idea to the Literary Army. Morina hopes the two will defeat each other so she can have the Otherworld all to herself.

SPECIES: Witch
BIRTHPLACE: The Charming Kingdom
OCCUPATION: Mistress of dark magic/potion maker
TRADEMARK: Manipulation
NEVER WITHOUT: Beauty potions

THE WITCHES

The witches live in hiding throughout the kingdoms but meet monthly in the Dwarf Forests during full moons. The most prominent witches among them are Serpentina, Tarantulene, Rat Mary, Charcoaline, and Arboris. The witches started out as normal women, but practicing black magic has given them each a unique

and foul appearance. They hope to conquer the Other-world so they can have their own world away from the Happily Forever After Assembly to control and terror-ize as they please.

SPECIES: Witch
BIRTHPLACE: Various
OCCUPATION: Mistresses of dark magic
TRADEMARK: Grotesqueness
NEVER WITHOUT: A victim

PLACES

to

GO

KINGDOMS
of the
FAIRY-TALE
WORLD

THE DWARF FORESTS

frightening and dangerous place, the Dwarf Forests are a territory without any laws or leadership. It's where people go when they don't want to be found. It's covered in thick and creepy forests and dark caves. It's the location Snow White ran to while trying to escape the Evil Queen and where Hansel and Gretel came across the gingerbread house.

THE CHARMING KINGDOM

he Charming Kingdom is a pleasant and peaceful country. It's made up of flowery meadows, a rolling countryside, and cottage homes. The most famous structure in the kingdom is the Charming Palace—the home of the Charming Dynasty. During a ball at the palace, Cinderella famously dances with Prince Chance Charming and then flees at the stroke of midnight.

THE NORTHERN KINGDOM

 he Northern Kingdom is a cold and icy country. It's covered in sharp mountain ranges and chilly bodies of water, including the Ugly Duckling Pond and Swan Lake. The Northern Kingdom was once ruled by the Evil Queen and is now the home of Queen Snow White and her husband, King Chandler Charming.

THE CENTER KINGDOM

he Center Kingdom was originally a group of farming communities in the Northern Kingdom. After a series of brutal wolf attacks, the people began the C.R.A.W.L. Revolution (Citizen Riots Against Wolf Liberty) until the Evil Queen granted them independence. The farmers built a protective wall around their country to keep out the wolves. They elected Red Riding Hood as their queen, and her first royal act was naming the nation the Red Riding Hood Kingdom. Years later the kingdom becomes known as the Bo Peep Republic, after Bo Peep beats Red Riding Hood in a surprise election. After Bo Peep's death, the country elects Froggy as its new leader. He renames the country the Center Kingdom to avoid any changes in the future.

THE EASTERN KINGDOM

Of all the kingdoms in the Land of Stories, the Eastern Kingdom has had the rockiest history. During the Dragon Age, the kingdom was covered in volcanoes and dragon nests. Centuries later, the Enchantress cursed the kingdom to sleep for a hundred years and covered it with her enchanted vines and thornbush. Once Queen Sleeping Beauty was awoken by Prince Chase Charming's kiss, she worked tirelessly to restore the kingdom to its former glory.

THE CORNER KINGDOM

The Corner Kingdom is a very quiet country ruled by Queen Rapunzel and her husband, Sir William. The land was once the property of a horrible witch who locked Rapunzel in a tower when she was just a girl. After the witch died, Rapunzel inherited the land and founded a kingdom for all the villages in the area.

THE ELF EMPIRE

The Elf Empire exists in the northwest corner of the Land of Stories. The entire population lives in homes scattered throughout the branches of an enormous tree. In the event that their home is threatened, the elves retreat to a hidden chamber located in the tree's roots. Although they were excluded from the Happily Ever After Assembly, Alex makes sure to include the elves and Empress Elvina when she forms the Happily Forever After Assembly.

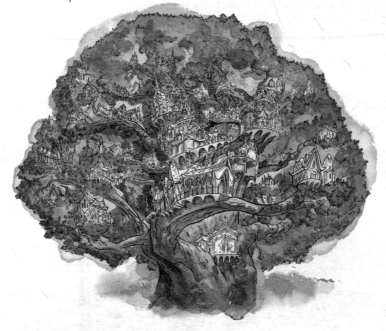

THE TROBLIN KINGDOM

any years ago, all the trolls and goblins throughout the kingdoms were banished to an underground territory for their crimes against humans and fairies. To unite the different species, the Troll and Goblin Territory was renamed the Troblin Kingdom when Queen Trollbella obtained the throne. During the Enchantress's reign of terror, the kingdom was flooded when Ezmia destroyed a dam protecting it from a strong river. The Troblins rebuilt their kingdom on floating platforms, and it became known as the Great Troblin Lake.

THE FAIRY KINGDOM

The Fairy Kingdom is the most beautiful and majestic of all the countries in the Land of Stories. It's covered in fantastical gardens and has breathtaking views of Mermaid Bay. The kingdom is home to several magical creatures, including herds of unicorns and flocks of pixies. The headquarters of the Happily Forever After Assembly is located in the Fairy Kingdom inside the golden Fairy Palace.

MERMAID BAY

Mermaid Bay is the home of the merpeople. It's a vast underwater kingdom that consists of colorful coral gardens, shipwrecks, and sunken palaces. Mermaid Bay's most famous resident was the Little Mermaid. After her death, the Little Mermaid became the Sea Foam Spirit, who watches over the merpeople and the ocean like a guardian angel.

THE CASTLE IN THE SKY

The Castle in the Sky is an enormous structure that sits in the clouds above the Center Kingdom. It was once the home of a terrifying giant, until he fell to his death chasing Jack down a magic beanstalk. To many people's surprise, the castle is still inhabited by the giant's enormous cat, whom Mother Goose named George Clooney.

WORLDS
BEYOND
the
KINGDOMS

OZ

*T*he *Wonderful Wizard of Oz* was written by L. Frank Baum and originally published in 1900. The Bailey twins and their friends travel to Oz using the Portal Potion to stop the Masked Man from recruiting the Wicked Witch of the West for his Literary Army. As they travel down the yellow brick road, they make friends with the Tin Woodman and Blubo the flying monkey while narrowly avoiding getting eaten by a pack of Kalidahs.

NEVERLAND

Neverland is a magical island floating in outer space in James M. Barrie's classic *Peter Pan*. It's home to pirates, mermaids, Native Americans, and a group of age-defying children. While the Masked Man recruits the dreadful Captain Hook and the crew of the *Jolly Roger* for his Literary Army, Peter Pan and the Lost Boys join the Bailey twins on their quest to save the fairy-tale world.

WONDERLAND

Wonderland is a world of mushroom forests, hookah-smoking caterpillars, and tardy white rabbits. The Bailey twins and their friends follow the Masked Man into Lewis Carroll's *Alice's Adventures in Wonderland* to stop him from recruiting the Queen of Hearts and her card soldiers for his Literary Army. Unfortunately, they aren't successful, and the Masked Man splits the twins and their friends into different literary dimensions.

CAMELOT

Camelot is the home of the legendary tale of King Arthur and Merlin. When Mother Goose and Alex arrive, Arthur is very young and Merlin is training him to become the future king of England. He and Merlin assist Alex and Mother Goose as they search for a way back into the Land of Stories. The more time that Alex and Mother Goose spend in the mythical story, the closer they become to the wizard and his squire, and *leaving* Camelot becomes much harder than either of them expected.

SHERWOOD FOREST

The Sherwood Forest is just outside Nottingham, England, and is home to the infamous outlaw Robin Hood. After befriending the thief and his gang of Merry Men, Conner and his friends must create their own batch of Portal Potion and defeat the menacing Sheriff of Nottingham before they can make it back to the Land of Stories.

CONNER'S SHORT STORIES

STARBOARDIA

"Starboardia" is a swashbuckling pirate adventure set in the high seas of the Caribbean. We follow Captain Auburn Sally and her all-female crew of the *Dolly Llama* as Admiral Jacobsen of the British Navy chases them across the ocean. Eventually the captain and the admiral must team up to stop a horrible gang of pirates led by the terrifying Smoky-Sails Sam. Greatly outnumbered, the captain and the admiral take their crews to the ancient island of Starboardia and use a complex structure to defeat the pirate once and for all.

GALAXY QUEEN

"Galaxy Queen" is an intergalactic space odyssey. With the help of Commander Newters and her cyborg army, the Cyborg Queen travels the universe and collects habitable planets for her home solar system. In exchange for the cyborgs' help to defeat their uncle, the Bailey twins strike a deal with the Cyborg Queen to exterminate a species of alien insects on a planet she has her eye on. The twins travel to Lollipopigust and exterminate the grotesque polycrabs—but the pests are a much *bigger* problem than they imagined.

THE ZIBLINGS

The Ziblings are a family of superheroes who live in the metropolis of Big City, USA. After an asteroid carrying cosmic radiation hits an unlucky orphanage, four children are left with remarkable superhuman abilities. Blaze has the power to control fire, Whipney can manipulate her hair, Morph can transform into anything his heart desires, and, although it takes him longer to master his gifts, Bolt has the power to fly and manifest lightning. A genius named Professor Wallet adopts the children and raises them to become a dynamic crime-fighting team.

THE ADVENTURES OF BLIMP BOY

"The Adventures of Blimp Boy" chronicles the archaeological voyages of Beau Rogers and his aunt Emgee as they travel the world in an enormous blimp. Set in the exploration days of the early twentieth century, the story follows Beau and Emgee as they obtain precious relics in the temples of India, the pyramids of Egypt, and beyond. However, preserving history comes at a high cost. Beau faces ferocious animals, primeval booby traps, and ancient curses as he collects the artifacts.

CEMETERY OF THE UNDEAD

"Cemetery of the Undead" is a short story written by Bree Campbell. The macabre tale is about a gravesite with tombs of the women Bree felt were wronged throughout history. But unlike other cemeteries, at the stroke of midnight all the corpses briefly come back to life! Historical figures like Marie-Antoinette, Anne Boleyn, and Joan of Arc creep out of their crypts and seek their revenge on unsuspecting visitors.

TRINKETS,
TREASURES,
and
ENCHANTMENTS

THE WISHING SPELL

The Wishing Spell is a legendary enchantment that grants someone a wish after a series of irreplaceable and invaluable items are collected. The items include Cinderella's glass slipper, Sleeping Beauty's spindle, jewels from Snow White's coffin, a lock of Rapunzel's hair, the Sea Witch's saber, the Troll and Goblin Kings' shared crown, the tears of a fairy, and a piece of Red Riding Hood's basket. During their first visit to the fairy-tale world, Alex and Conner collect the Wishing Spell items hoping to wish for a way home. Unfortunately, the Evil Queen beats them to it.

These were the clues to the ingredients that Alex and Conner had to find:

GLASS THAT HOUSED A LONELY SOUL UP
'TIL MIDNIGHT'S FINAL TOLL.
A SABER FROM THE DEEPEST SEA,
MEANT FOR A GROOM'S MORTALITY.
THE BARK OF A BASKET HELD IN FRIGHT WHILE
RUNNING FROM A BARK WITH BITE.
A STONY CROWN THAT'S MADE TO SHARE,
FOUND DEEP WITHIN A SAVAGE LAIR.
A NEEDLE THAT PIERCED THE LOVELY SKIN OF
A PRINCESS WITH BEAUTY FOUND WITHIN.
A WAVY LOCK OF GOLDEN ROPE THAT ONCE
WAS FREEDOM'S ONLY HOPE.
GLITTERING JEWELS WHOSE VALUE INCREASED
AFTER PRESERVING THE FALSE DECEASED.
TEARDROPS OF A MAIDEN FAIRY FEELING
NEITHER MAGICAL NOR MERRY.

THE WAND OF WONDERMENT

The Wand of Wonderment is the most powerful magic wand in the history of the fairy-tale world and grants invincibility to whoever is holding it. The wand was constructed from the most prized possessions of the six most hated people in the kingdoms. In order to stop the evil Enchantress, the Bailey twins and their friends travel through the Land of Stories collecting the Snow Queen's icicle scepter, the Sea Witch's black pearl necklace, the Wicked Stepmother's wedding ring, the giant's golden harp, shards of the Evil Queen's Magic Mirror, and, most difficult to obtain: the pride from the Enchantress herself.

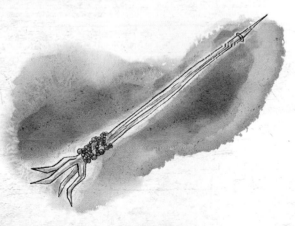

MAGIC
MIRRORS

Imprisoning someone inside a magic mirror takes extremely powerful magic, and it's also one of the cruelest acts. People who find themselves in the mirror dimension have the power to appear in any mirror in the world, but the ability comes at a great cost. The longer someone is trapped inside a magic mirror, the more memories and sense of self they lose. Soon the prisoners fade into nothing but the reflections of the world around them.

MIRRORS OF TRUTH

A Mirror of Truth does not show a physical reflection, but the reflection of who someone is on the inside. The most beautiful women in the world would see a hideous monster staring back at them if they had a wicked spirit. The most powerful men would see a spoiled little boy if they didn't rule justly. During their trip to the fairy-tale world, Alex and Conner first learn they have magic in their blood from a Mirror of Truth.

THE PORTAL AT NEUSCHWANSTEIN CASTLE

In the early 1800s, the Grande Armée forced the Brothers Grimm and Mother Goose to take them into the fairy-tale world. Mother Goose bewitched a portal in Bavaria to trap the soldiers for more than two hundred years. She then asked her friend King Ludwig II to build a fairy-tale-like castle around the portal to trick the Grande Armée into thinking they had traveled to the fairy-tale world in case they ever resurfaced. To this day, a portal to the Land of Stories exists inside the music hall of Neuschwanstein Castle and can be activated if the right melody is played on a magic panpipe.

THE SOUTH BANK LION

During the mid-1800s, Mother Goose had a difficult time making friends when she visited England. So the senior spitfire magically brought a lion statue on top of her favorite brewery company to life. During her routine visits over the centuries, Mother Goose confessed all of her secrets to the lion, giving him the concerned expression he wears today. The South Bank Lion statue can be found in central London down the street from Big Ben, but it's recommended not to mention Mother Goose while you're in his presence—the poor thing has been traumatized enough.

MOTHER GOOSE'S VAULT

eep underground beneath the Lumière des Etoiles
casino in Monte Carlo is a secret storage facility.
The facility is hundreds of years old and home to thousands of vaults leased by some of the most mysterious
people on earth. Mother Goose keeps all the memen-
tos she's collected throughout her years of visiting the
Otherworld in vault 317. George Washington's dentures,
a map to Atlantis, the Holy Grail, and Amelia Earhart's
forwarding address are some of the many objects she
keeps safely out of public view.

THE HALL OF DREAMS

The Hall of Dreams is a magical chamber inside the Fairy Palace. It's an infinite space containing millions of bubbles that represent people's hopes and dreams. By looking into a bubble, the Fairy Godmother can see someone's greatest desire and help them achieve it. Unfortunately, after the Grande Armée attacks the fairy-tale world, people's spirits drastically sink and the majority of the bubbles disappear. Alex and Conner make it their mission to restore the Hall of Dreams by restoring people's faith.

DRAGON EGGS

In order for a dragon to hatch, the egg must be submerged in extremely hot temperatures, which is why many mothers made their nests inside volcanoes during the Dragon Age. Once the egg hatches, the infant's growth depends on the amount it feeds. The more it eats, the faster it grows. A dragon forms a bond with whatever oversees its hatching and feeding, most commonly its mother, but humans have been known to raise and train dragons, too.

THE
PORTAL POTION

The Portal Potion is a magical serum that creates a portal into the world of any written work it touches. The ingredients include a lock and key from a loved one, a feather from the finest pheasant, a branch from the tallest tree, a considerable amount of moonlight, and a touch of magic. Alex and Conner are forced to make their own concoctions when the Masked Man splits them up in the worlds of Camelot and the Sherwood Forest.

THE BRIDGE
BETWEEN WORLDS

For thousands of years, the Otherworld and the Land of Stories have been spinning around the sun in different dimensions. Since the Otherworld moves much faster than the fairy-tale world, the two collide every so often, momentarily opening a gateway between them. As the Sisters Grimm follow the coordinates and the timing of the collisions, they make a startling discovery—*the worlds are set to collide and connect indefinitely*! Unfortunately, it gives the witches and the Literary Army a chance to enter the Otherworld and conquer it. Alex and Conner eventually condense the bridge into a book, *The Land of Stories: Volume Two*, which they put into the trusting hands of President Katherine Walker.

BONUS CHAPTERS

CONSPIRACIST CONTAGION

Mrs. Peters was starting to regret accepting her recent promotion to high school principal. It was half past noon, and the veteran educator was already having an impossibly difficult day. She was in the middle of a call with a very unhappy custodian, and she was glad they were speaking by phone so he couldn't see her agitated expression.

"I understand the horse made a huge mess in the student parking lot," Mrs. Peters said. "Ms. Miller's car broke down this morning and the horse was the only feasible way she could get to school on time. I will ask her to help you clean it up after school, but I don't think it's fair to punish a student after going to such extremes to keep her perfect attendance."

Her receptionist knocked on her door and peeked into her office.

"Mrs. Peters, there's a group of young women here who would like to speak to you," she said.

"Please tell them I'm on the phone," Mrs. Peters said.

The receptionist's eyes grew large, and the principal could sense a hint of fear behind them. "I tried," she said. "But they're being very *persistent*."

Suddenly, Mindy pushed the receptionist out of her way and barged into the office. Cindy, Lindy, and Wendy quickly filed in behind her. It was a freshman ambush.

"We have waited long enough!" Mindy said with a raised voice. "It's time someone around here gave us some answers, and we're not leaving until we get them!"

Her face was flushed and she paced around the office in a temper.

Mrs. Peters sighed. "Stan, I'm going to have to call you back," she told the custodian, and hung up the phone. "Girls, have a seat."

Mindy sat in the chair across from the desk and the other girls stood around her like bodyguards. All four of them crossed their arms and glared at the principal.

"What can I help you with, ladies?" she asked. "Is everything all right with the Reading Club? Wait, forgive me, I meant the Book Hugging Club."

"We're not the Book Huggers anymore," Cindy said.

"We're the *Conspiracy Club* now," Lindy said.

"You would have known that if *someone* passed along our e-mail like she *said* she would," Mindy said, and shot the receptionist a dirty look.

The receptionist slowly tiptoed out of the room, leaving Mrs. Peters alone with the aggressive girls.

"I didn't realize you four were interested in conspiracies," Mrs. Peters said.

Mindy squinted intensely. "We are now," she said. "And we think you know why."

"I do?" Mrs. Peters asked. The Conspiracy Club's members nodded in agreement, although the principal had no clue what they were getting at.

"Alex and Conner Bailey," Lindy said, and pointed at her. *"We know you know the truth!"*

"The truth?" Mrs. Peters asked.

"About what really happened to them!" Cindy said.

Mrs. Peters blinked awkwardly at them. Had she missed something?

"Miss Bailey is living in Vermont with a relative, and Mr. Bailey is being homeschooled," she said.

Mindy rose from the chair and slammed her hands on the desk. *"LIES!"* she yelled.

"Ms. Morris, control yourself or I'll have you escorted out of my office!" Mrs. Peters said.

Mindy quickly sat back down. "I'm sorry, Mrs. Peters," she said. "Not knowing the truth is like a poison. We know something strange is going on with the Bailey twins, but no one will talk to us."

"We've filed police reports, we've consulted private investigators, and we've even reached out to the FBI!" Cindy said.

"Everyone only laughs at us," Lindy said.

Mrs. Peters shook her head in disbelief. "Girls, what exactly do you think happened to the Bailey twins?"

The Conspiracy Club's members eyed one another. Lindy and Cindy went to the windows and closed the blinds. Wendy shut the door to prevent any eavesdropping. Mindy leaned across the desk as far as she could without climbing it.

"Based on all the evidence we've gathered, we believe they've been captured by *cross-dimensional beings*," Mindy said in total seriousness.

Mrs. Peters had never raised her eyebrows so high. "Cross-dimensional beings?" she asked. "What on earth made you come to that conclusion?"

Mindy got to her feet again and paced around the room. "It all started four years ago," she explained. "Times were simpler back then; you were just a sixth-grade teacher, and we were just your students. Do you recall a two-week period when Alex and Conner were absent from class?"

"If memory serves me correctly, they had the chicken pox," Mrs. Peters said.

Mindy laughed. "Chicken pox?" she said. "That's funny, because usually you can tell if someone has had chicken pox. Isn't that right, *Wendy*?"

Wendy put her foot on top of the desk and pulled back her pant leg. Her skin was covered in tiny faded scars.

"Now, *that's* the aftermath of chicken pox," Mindy said. "And yet the Bailey twins returned without a single blemish on their skin. One year later, the Bailey twins were absent again, this time for almost a month! And, mysteriously, Alex never returned."

"I remember that quite well," Mrs. Peters said. "They were visiting a relative in Vermont. Alex stayed there to attend a school for advanced learners. I thought it was a rather odd departure, too, but I had to respect her and her mother's wishes."

"You know what else was odd? Alex's behavior shortly before she left!" Mindy said. "Every day at lunch, she would go into the library and pull the same book off the shelf. She held it close to her body and whispered sweet nothings into its spine, like '*I want to go back*' or '*Please take me away*.' It was like she was talking to someone!"

"As if her wish was granted, a couple weeks later *Alex disappeared*!" Lindy said.

"Last year, we cornered Conner on the plane to Germany and asked him about it," Mindy said. "In an obvious cover-up, he acted like we were crazy and refused to give us an honest answer."

"Then history repeated itself, because a few days into the trip, *Conner vanished*!" Lindy said.

"He didn't vanish," Mrs. Peters said. "It was very unlike Conner to run off like he and Ms. Campbell did. His mother was very concerned about his behavior, so she decided to homeschool him."

Cindy looked like it was the most ridiculous thing she had ever heard. "Homeschool? *Homeschool,* she says!"

"But did you ever *see* him again physically with your own eyes?" Lindy asked.

"Um...no," Mrs. Peters said. "But I don't believe his mother would have a reason to lie to me."

"We tried to get the truth out of Bree Campbell, but to no surprise, she couldn't give us a straight answer, either," Mindy said. "We caught her making a secret phone call in the janitors' closet. It was hard to hear her conversation, even with the empty glasses we used, but we did hear the word *blood* many times."

"*Blood,* Mrs. Peters! Why would a fifteen-year-old girl be making secret phone calls about blood?" Cindy said.

"And during school hours, no less!" Lindy said.

"*Where did Alex really go? What actually happened to Conner? And why is Bree talking about blood in closets?*" Mindy asked, in hysterics. "*These are the questions that haunt our dreams!*"

Mrs. Peters took off her glasses and massaged her eyes. In over thirty years of working in education, she had never dealt with something quite like this.

"Well, you've convinced me of one thing," Mrs. Peters said.

"What?" the girls asked in unison.

"I need to retire," Mrs. Peters said.

The Conspiracy Club's members exchanged guilty looks. This had never been their intention. "Mrs. Peters, you can't retire at a time like this! We need your help uncovering the truth!" Mindy pleaded.

"Then your next principal will have to help you," she said. "I've been working in education for over three decades—I'm too tired to deal with the ever-growing and eccentric needs of teenagers today. It's a reality I've struggled to realize until this moment."

"But what about the Bailey twins?" Cindy asked.

They looked up at Mrs. Peters with wide eyes oozing with desperation.

"Let me give you some advice," the principal said. "Let's pretend your assumptions are right and the Bailey twins did get abducted by something otherworldly—I can't imagine there would be a way you could prove it. So rather than wasting all this energy trying to solve the impossible, why don't you relax and *enjoy the mystery?* Your generation is so wrapped up in technology, and social media, and instant gratification, you don't realize that ignorance is bliss. Sometimes *not knowing* is more fun."

The Conspiracy Club's members all collectively slumped. They were a little embarrassed at how far they had taken their theories.

"You know, it would be nice to have a good night's sleep," Mindy said.

"My 4.0 GPA has slipped down to 3.98," Cindy said. "I never thought an obsession would be so time-consuming."

"To be honest, I've been neglecting my pets," Lindy said. "Now I get why my gerbil has been so moody lately."

Mrs. Peters smiled at them. "You see, there are so many other facets to your lives that are more deserving of your attention."

"It might be nice to start *reading* again." Mindy shrugged.

"Yeah, I miss reading!" Cindy said.

"It sure was less stressful than solving conspiracies," Lindy said.

"Then is it safe to say the Reading Club has returned?" Mrs. Peters asked.

The girls shared a smile and nodded. The Book Huggers were back.

"Thanks, Mrs. Peters," Mindy said. "I hope we didn't actually drive you to retirement."

Mrs. Peters laughed. "You were just a drop in the ocean, dear," she said. "Now I think it's time you went back to class."

The Book Huggers moseyed out of her office, each feeling a little lighter than when they entered. However, their time together had the opposite effect on their principal. Mrs. Peters stared off into space in total silence for the rest of the afternoon. The more she thought about their conversation, the more she started to believe their paranoia might have been warranted.

Retirement wasn't the only thing the Book Huggers had persuaded her of; Mrs. Peters was now consumed with suspicions of her own about the Bailey twins....

the
NIGHT SHIFT

Unbeknownst to most tourists who visit Manhattan, the city's great Central Park is the home of a small castle. Belvedere Castle sits in the middle of the park between Turtle Pond and Seventy-Ninth Street and is made of gray bricks and covered in ivy. The castle acts as a visitor center and offers spectacular views of the lawns and skyscrapers surrounding the park.

It was built in 1869 and designed by Frederick Law Olmsted and Calvert Vaux. Since the early 1900s, the National Weather Service has measured the speed and direction of wind with instruments installed in the castle's tallest tower. However, most important for the sake of this story is that the castle was cleaned three nights a week by a janitor named Rusty Bagdasarian.

Every Monday, Wednesday, and Friday evening, Rusty would leave his home in Brooklyn at nine o'clock and take the train into the city. From ten o'clock to four in the morning, he swept the stone floors, washed the stained-glass windows, and sang along to his favorite songs on the radio. The large open rooms and solid walls gave a nice reverb, convincing Rusty he was far more vocally gifted than he actually was.

At the end of every shift, Rusty climbed up to the castle's tallest tower and looked out over Central Park and the city beyond it with pride. No matter how many times he saw the stunning view, it never lost an ounce of its splendor. As far as Rusty was concerned, New York City was the most magnificent place in the world. It was a city of concrete, lights, dreams, opportunities, and life, and the janitor felt lucky to be a part of it.

Naturally, working nights in Central Park had its downside. Occasionally Rusty would find a homeless person sleeping inside the castle or catch a gang of delinquents defacing it, but never anything a quick call to the police couldn't solve. It wasn't until a particular Monday night that Rusty witnessed the most bizarre thing he had ever encountered—in the castle and in his life.

It was five minutes after one AM, and Rusty was cleaning the windows. He belted out the lyrics to a song on his radio that was sung by a pop princess about breaking up with a famous actor.

"You're oh-so-Hollywood, like every bad boy should— but what you didn't see, was that you needed meeee!" Rusty sang along, oblivious to everything but the lyrics and the windows. *"You've got that soap-star pout, that most girls dream about—but what you cannot say, is that, boy, you're—"*

Suddenly, a soft vibration traveled through the castle. It pulsated, growing stronger and stronger until the entire castle rattled. Rusty took cover under the nearest table, but the tremor lasted only a few moments.

"Must have been an earthquake," Rusty said to himself.

He did a quick walk-through of the castle to make sure no damage had been done and then returned to the windows and his song. At the end of his shift, he locked up the castle and headed home, passing a homeless man on his way to the subway station.

"Quite an earthquake earlier, huh?" Rusty asked.

"What earthquake?" the man said.

"The one that happened a couple hours ago," Rusty explained. "You didn't feel it?"

"All I felt was a nasty headache brought on by your terrible singing!" he said.

The homeless man was only a few yards away from the castle—how could he not have felt it? Rusty figured he must have slept through it, or maybe was a bit delusional. When Rusty got home, he flipped through the morning news programs, but there was no mention of an earthquake on any of the stations.

"I must have imagined it," he decided, and didn't spend any more time thinking about it.

A few weeks later, on another Monday night shortly after one o'clock in the morning, Rusty was back at work sweeping the floors of the castle while he listened to his radio. A song came on by a young man who sang like he was going through puberty, but the lyrics were so catchy, Rusty couldn't help singing along.

"You give me diabetes, because your love is so sweet— girl, you are my insulin, without you I'm incomplete! My heart keeps break-break-breaking, and I keep drink-drink- drinking, can't stop eat-eat-eating, because I'm think- think-thinking, about yooou, baby—"

Just as it had a few weeks before, a light vibration filled the castle. It grew stronger with every pulsation, each becoming twice as strong as the previous one. Rusty was so surprised that he didn't shield himself. He just watched the castle quivering around him, knowing it definitely wasn't a hallucination this time. It lasted twice as long as it had before, and as soon as it ended, Rusty dialed the police.

"New York Police Department," a woman answered.

"Hello, I'm calling to report…well, an *earthquake*," he said.

"An earthquake? Sir, usually people don't report earthquakes."

"I understand, but this isn't the first time I've experi- enced it, and I figured someone should know about it," Rusty said. "I work nights at Belvedere Castle in Central Park, and I believe it may be on top of a very active fault line."

"Sir, we get these kinds of calls all the time," the woman said calmly. "What you're experiencing is a train passing underground beneath you."

Rusty felt like a complete moron. He took the subway to work every day, yet it had never crossed his mind.

"Right," he said. "That must be what it is. Forgive me for calling. Have a nice night."

Rusty got off the phone and had a good laugh at his own paranoia.

That night on his way home, a subway map on the wall of the station caught his eye as he waited for his train. He inspected it and traced all the routes through the city, but there didn't appear to be a track that went under Central Park anywhere near Belvedere Castle.

When his train arrived, he approached the front car and tapped on the operator's window.

"Can I help you?" the operator asked.

"Yes. Do you by chance know of any trains that travel below Central Park near Belvedere Castle?" Rusty asked.

"Belvedere Castle?" the operator asked.

"Yes, it's between Seventy-Ninth Street and Turtle Pond," Rusty said.

The operator looked over a similar map on the wall behind him.

"Doesn't look like the subway goes under that part of the park," the operator said. "Why do you ask?"

"Oh, no reason," Rusty said. "Thank you."

His original hunch must have been correct—the castle probably sat right on top of a fault line.

The next day, Rusty went to the library and found a massive book on plate tectonics. It had maps of all the existing fault lines beneath New York. He traced the map with his finger, expecting to find one right below Central Park—but there were none remotely close to the castle.

Rusty paced around his apartment for the rest of the day, trying to figure out what else could be causing the tremors in the castle. Before he pursued anyone else's help about the matter, Rusty figured it would be good to have proof.

He purchased an old video camera from a thrift store. Every night he worked at the castle, he placed the camera on a shelf and left it recording as he cleaned around it. For weeks and weeks, Rusty recorded every moment of his shifts, with no luck.

Over time, Rusty lost interest and stopped bringing his camera to work. He figured the earthquakes—or whatever they had been—had just been rare phenomena and probably wouldn't return. Then, late one Friday night, as he wiped the railings of the main balcony, he discovered he was wrong.

Unlike the previous instances, there was no soft vibration to warn him. Belvedere Castle violently shook as if it were inside a giant snow globe. Rusty was almost knocked off the balcony, and he desperately held on to the railing. The quake was three times as strong as the first one, and a large crack traveled across the balcony floor. A few windows in the towers shattered, raining shards of glass over the terrified janitor.

Rusty looked around the castle in a panic and saw a bright flash just a few feet in the air above the balcony. At first he thought it had been caused by something electrical—perhaps the weather instruments in the tower had been damaged. Then, suddenly, just for a split second, he could have sworn he saw a thick and endless forest replace the view of New York City around the castle—but before he realized what he was looking at, the forest was gone and the city reappeared.

Eventually the rumbling stopped, but Rusty was too afraid to move, and he continued clutching the railing. Whatever he had experienced was definitely not earthquakes. Rusty feared the tremors were just the beginning of something much worse and more complex headed for Belvedere Castle....

GOOSE/ COLFER:
the INTERVIEW *of a* LIFETIME

moderated by MOTHER GOOSE

Hello to all the wonderful readers of the Land of Stories series and the parents who buy books for them! Mother Goose here—the senior citizen most likely to be under a citizen's arrest!

Recently, I took a trip to Las Vegas with my favorite literary sorcerer, Merlin (hands off, ladies, the wizard's mine!). In between playing card games and slot machines and running from loan sharks, Merlin and I took a stroll down a row of shops and passed a bookstore (although I don't know who has time to read in Sin City). Wouldn't you know it, displayed in the window were the Land of Stories books by Chris Colfer.

Well, I was just floored! I couldn't believe the pasty little boy the fairies and I met two decades ago had managed to turn our stories into a bestselling series! Regardless of their success, I thought his books could use a little *oomph*. So, to help him out, I decided to put together this editorial piece to get the attention of new readers.

I met up with Chris at his home in Los Angeles to talk about everything related to the Land of Stories series and ask him the questions on every twelve-year-old's mind. Little did I know it would be the greatest journalistic endeavor since Frost/Nixon (look it up, kids). Our discussion went as follows.

MOTHER GOOSE: Howdy, Chris! Thanks for taking the time out of your busy schedule to have a chat with me!

CHRIS COLFER: How did you get inside my house?

MG: This is *your* house? Good lord, I thought we were in Queen Victoria's tearoom. Has anyone ever told you that you decorate like an old woman?

CC: As a matter of fact, I— *Wait! Who are you?*

MG: Really, Chris? Is *that* how you greet your favorite muse?

CC: Oh my God…*You're Mother Goose!* This can't be real! I must have hit my head or something!

MG: As I said to Howard Hughes, *no, you're not dreaming, I'm really here.* And no offense, but I'd like to get to my questions, if you don't mind wiping that look of shock off your face.

CC: Okay…What kind of questions?

MG: We asked readers from all over the globe to send in questions for their favorite author. Sadly, J. K. Rowling was unavailable to answer them. *Ba-dum-bum!*

CC: Was that supposed to be funny?

MG: No, that was supposed to be *very* funny. Anyhoo, fans of the Land of Stories series sent in their questions for you, but all of them were terribly boring, so I've composed a list of my own. Are you ready?

CC: I feel like I should have a representative present.

MG: *Question number one*: What gives you the right to write about so many characters who don't belong to you?

CC: Actually, every character I use in the Land of Stories is either my own or is in the public domain.

MG: *Whoa, buddy!* I'm gonna stop you right there. I may be a public enemy, but I am *not* public domain.

CC: I'm not sure what you *think* it is, but public domain means I can legally use characters that are no longer copyrighted.

MG: I've always found the *law* to be more of a suggestion, haven't you?

CC: No.

MG: Well, if I followed the law, your books wouldn't be nearly as interesting. Speaking of which, that brings me to *question number two*: I think you owe me some money for publishing my diary.

CC: That's not a question.

MG: You don't need a question mark when something is questionable. You're lucky there are so many warrants out for my arrest; otherwise, I'd see you in court.

CC: What are you talking about? I wrote every word of *The Mother Goose Diaries* myself. Just like I wrote every word of all my other books.

MG: Don't get all defensive on me, Richard Nixon. I'm not accusing you of having a ghostwriter, but maybe you're getting more *"interdimensional help"* than you realize.

CC: What's that supposed to mean?

MG: Allow me to explain. When did you first start writing the Land of Stories series?

CC: I was in second or third grade.

MG: Exactly. That's a curious activity for a seven-year-old, wouldn't you say?

CC: Well, I was too young for Boy Scouts, and I was kicked off my T-ball team. I needed *something* to do.

MG: And that's precisely why the other fairies and I decided you were the best person to tell the Bailey twins' story. We took one look at you and thought, *Now, there's a kid with a lot of time on his hands.*

CC: Hold on. Are you telling me the Land of Stories isn't my creation?

MG: Something like that.

CC: But that's not true! The series was inspired by the questions I had about fairy-tale characters when I was a kid and the adventures I wanted to have in the fairy-tale world!

MG: Don't get your tail feathers in a twist. I'm merely suggesting that we planted the seed. But don't worry— you, and only you, were the manure that helped it grow.

CC: Thanks?

MG: Let's try to get back to the interview—I've got a deadline to make.

CC: This is being *published*?

MG: Well, look who's talking! It's not fun to have stuff about your personal life published without your permission, is it?

CC: [*Sigh.*] Next question, please.

MG: *Question number three*: Why do you always write me like I'm some crazy old lush?

CC: Because you reference people like Howard Hughes and you *just* spilled your bubbly all over my rug. I'd say it's pretty fitting.

MG: This is sparkling mineral water, thank you very much. *Question number four*: I read somewhere that you were an actor before you became an author.

CC: That sounded more like a judgment than a question.

MG: It was. Usually people pick a career in medicine or business to fall back on. With your chosen professions, it's like you decided to sail upstream without a paddle *or* a canoe.

CC: Well, performing and writing have always been the same thing to me. You get to be a *storyteller* in both fields, and at the end of the day, I suppose a storyteller is what I consider myself the most.

MG: Well, *la-di-da*. I know what you mean, though.

I was an actress myself back in the golden days of Hollywood—you know, before all this *streaming* trash.

CC: Would I recognize your work?

MG: Did you ever see the film *Gone with the Wind*?

CC: Of course!

MG: I supplied the wind.

CC: [*A beat of silence.*] How much longer is this interview going to take?

MG: *Question number five*: Would you ever consider cowriting something with another author? Personally, I've got a manuscript of a spicy romance novel I'd love to slap your name on. It's called *Fifty Shades of Goose*.

CC: I just threw up a little in the back of my mouth.

MG: So, you'll consider it. *Question number six*: You've said *The Land of Stories: Worlds Collide* is the last book in the series. But that doesn't mean the Land of Stories is over, does it?

CC: Why did you wink at me when you asked that?

MG: I did no such thing.

CC: You just did it again! You winked at me like you know something I don't!

MG: Maybe there's more to the story we just haven't told you yet. Maybe while you're asleep tonight, the fairies and I will fill your subconscious with images of all the crazy events that happened to the Bailey twins in their twenties.

CC: Actually, there is something you can fill me in on.

MG: What's that?

CC: In the last chapter of *Worlds Collide*, you asked Conner to go to your Monte Carlo vault and flush a brown paper bag hidden in the corner.

MG: And?

CC: Well, I'm curious. What was in the brown paper bag?

MG: I'm sorry, but that's all the time we have for today. Thank you so much for joining us, Chris. Best of luck as you continue to recklessly sail up that stream.

CC: Yes, thank you so much! If you have half as much fun reading my books as I've had writing them, then my mission is complete.

MG: Please know the hypercritical descriptions of the characters found in the novels are the author's views and *only* the author's views—especially those he describes as "elderly" and "intoxicated."

CC: I only use those adjectives when I'm describing your—

MG: Good night, folks! And in case I don't see you again, have yourselves a *happily ever after*!

Cheers!

Mother
Goose

CHRIS'S SECRETS *from the* LAND *of* STORIES

Over the years, I've been asked a thousand times who or what inspired the characters in the Land of Stories series. For the most part, I've remained very coy about answering and have only hinted at inspirations here and there. As amusing as it's been to keep readers guessing, I've decided to put the Book Huggers out of their misery and finally confess which persons, places, and things helped me imagine the people of the fairy-tale world. *It's time to spill the lily pad tea!*

the

HEROES

ALEX AND CONNER BAILEY

My zodiac sign is Gemini, and that means I'm constantly thinking and feeling two things at once. Having a Leo ascendant and a moon in Cancer does me absolutely no favors in that area. For anyone who isn't an astrology nerd, that simply means I'm never afraid to show my claws when I need to, but I'll always feel bad about it later. Sound familiar?

The Bailey twins represent my unique brand of crazy and the perspectives it gave me as a kid. The conversations between Alex and Conner are based on the arguments I have with myself on a daily basis. One side of me is always fixing to make a joke, while the other side is desperately aiming for productivity. In short, Conner is my brain and Alex is my heart.

When I first tried writing the Land of Stories in second grade, the twins' names were Max and Amy—named after my Mighty Max action figure and my cousin Amy. Later, I tragically lost Max during a trip to the grocery store with my mom. It was a really sore subject, so I changed the name to Conner after the character I played in a community-theater production of *Dad's Christmas Miracle*. That year, my cousin Amy called me a horrible name that was unforgivable (cacapoopyface, I believe it was). So I ditched Amy and named the heroine after the only cousin who hadn't disappointed me yet—a newborn named Alex.

From that moment on, whenever I daydreamed about the fairy-tale world, I always imagined it through Alex's and Conner's eyes.

FROGGY

My grandmother Fawnda has a fridge covered in dozens of magnets dating back to the seventies. A magnet that caught my attention as a child was an adorable frog head. Froggy, as I christened him, had big glossy eyes and a wide smile. My cousins and I used to place him over one another's school portraits as a joke which was hysterical until it happened to you. One day I walked into her kitchen and saw that Froggy had been placed over my uncle's wedding picture—and there, right before my eyes, was *a frog in a three-piece suit*! I found it so amusing that I immediately put him in the Land of Stories and I write about the classy amphibian to this day.

The year *The Land of Stories: The Wishing Spell* was published, my aunts discovered the frog magnet while they were spring-cleaning my grandmother's house. Had I not walked into the kitchen at that exact moment, they would have thrown him in the trash. I cleaned him up and filled in his cracks with a green Sharpie, and Froggy's been on the file cabinet in my office ever since.

RED

There are a number of people I've always *thought* inspired Red (family members I roll my eyes at, actresses I've worked with, socialites I've avoided, etc.). However, my friends are always very quick to point out the similarities that Red bears to *me*.

"You *literally* live in a house surrounded by a wall with signs that tell people to leave you alone. How many more comparisons do you need?"

However misguided my friends may be, Red has always been the character who surprises people the most, so I try to take the comparison as a compliment. On the surface, she seems like a ditzy, attention-seeking spoiled brat—but as we get to know her, we learn it's all a misinterpretation of her personality. Red isn't dumb; the world just doesn't know how to appreciate her brand of intelligence yet. She can't be pretentious when she *genuinely* believes everything she says. And she can't be selfish if she thinks her priorities benefit *everyone*. So if those are the qualities my friends recognize in both the queen and me, then I'm proud to say Red lives inside of me as much as the Bailey twins do.

"You *also* form opinions before knowing any facts."

That one I can't dispute.

GOLDILOCKS

As you've probably noticed by now, I've got a soft spot for strong female characters. When I was a kid, I always preferred the heroines over the heroes in all the books I read and movies I watched. Male protagonists are usually quite arrogant and self-righteous; they're only slaying the dragon to *prove* or *gain* something. Whereas female protagonists are usually quite *selfless*; they slay dragons to keep the peace or return a kingdom to its former glory. And usually the heroine has already had to fight for acceptance long before the hero even shows up—now, *that's* a person I think most people can identify with.

One of my favorite television shows growing up was *Xena: Warrior Princess*. I loved Xena's courage, her fearlessness, and her ability to take down opponents regardless of their gender, size, or immortality. Goldilocks embodies all those qualities, and I love how readers have responded to her. She's the favorite character of both little boys and little girls across the country—which I'm very proud of.

I'll also never forget the time a little girl said to me, "Thanks for making the girls just as strong as the boys." I wish we lived in a world where she didn't feel the need to thank me.

JACK

Whenever I write about Jack, I always picture the big brother I wish I had. Since Jack famously had a rough childhood (he and his mother were dirt-poor), I figured he learned early in life to never sweat the small stuff. So, unlike a lot of male literary characters, Jack doesn't try to dominate situations or tell others what to do—he just goes with the flow, even when the helm is being steered by twelve-year-olds. Jack is unconditional love and support personified, there's not an ounce of ego or malice in his body, and he'd do anything to protect his friends and family. I love writing about Jack because I believe the world could use more men like him.

CHARLOTTE BAILEY

J ust like Charlotte, my own mother was a redhead and worked in medicine. She wore blue scrubs to work every day and was usually on the phone with a coworker when I arrived home from school—hence the scene in the second chapter of *The Wishing Spell* where we meet Charlotte. At dinner, my mother would always talk about the surgeries she participated in that day at the hospital (in *graphic* detail, no less!) while our family was eating. I ultimately decided to spare the Bailey twins from this morbid ritual—they had been through enough already.

THE FAIRY GODMOTHER

The twins' grandmother is based on my late grand-mother, Patricia. Whenever our grandma Pat would visit, she'd bring a new storybook to read to my sister and me. She'd also happily play games with us—even if it meant crawling across the couches in a heated round of "hot lava." She also never *told* anyone when she was visit-ing, so her spontaneous arrivals felt quite magical as a kid.

My grandmother worked as a receptionist in the office of an elementary school—but she rarely stayed at her desk. Whenever the principals needed her, they always found her sitting on the floor in the waiting area, reading storybooks to the students. When she passed away, the school installed bookshelves and dedicated that section of the office to my grandmother with a plaque that read PAT'S CORNER.

MOTHER GOOSE

There's nothing I love more in the entire world than a crass old lady with stories to tell. Mother Goose is based on all the older women I'm lucky enough to have in my life, in particular my late friend Polly Bergen. She played my grandmother in an independent film I wrote called *Struck By Lightning*. And at eighty-two years old, she was dancing, drinking, spilling secrets, and playing Nintendo at our film's premiere. I used to sit and listen to her stories about 1950s politics and Hollywood for hours and hours. I'll never forget the moment she picked up her buzzing cell phone, read the caller ID, and said, "Oh, it's just Nancy Reagan. I'll call her back later."

TROLLBELLA

My little sister, Hannah, was the main inspiration for Trollbella. Just like the troll queen, my sister is totally boy crazy and can negotiate her way into anything. I've always described Trollbella as having the heart of a fangirl but the authority of a supreme dictator—which is a dangerous combination for teenage boy bands. I also love how different Trollbella is from the rest of her kingdom, yet it's *her* ideas and leadership that bring the trolls and goblins into prosperity.

EMERELDA AND
THE FAIRY COUNCIL

E merelda is based on my fabulous friend Pam—one
of very few people I've met with an enormous heart
and a powerful job. I've always been inspired by Pam's
unique mixture of compassion and responsibility, and
Emerelda is a tribute to her.

It was very important to me to maintain the classic
imagery in the stories by the Brothers Grimm, Charles
Perrault, and Hans Christian Andersen, *but* even more
important to have diversity—which doesn't always exist
in fairy-tale adaptions. The Fairy Council was the perfect way to feature characters of different ethnicities,
LGBTQIA characters, and characters with disabilities in
the series who could play a vital role in the plot of each
book.

the

VILLAINS

THE EVIL QUEEN

Ever since *Wicked*, I've been obsessed with backstories and knew I had to give one to the Evil Queen. In the time since *The Wishing Spell* was first published, Snow White's infamous stepmother has been portrayed in numerous movies, novels, and television shows. But I have to admit, *my take on the Evil Queen is still my favorite!*

To all the aspiring writers who read my books and hope to write backstories for their own villains one day, I have this advice: A *good* backstory makes us *feel sorry* for a villain, but a *great* backstory makes us *identify* with the villain.

However, since *The Wishing Spell* was my first novel, I wasn't able to describe the meaning behind her heart of stone as well as I could today. In the story, Evly has a witch cut her heart out of her chest and turn it into stone so she no longer feels the pain of missing Mira, the man trapped in her Magic Mirror. It's a macabre arc for a macabre character, but it was meant as a commentary on the people who *numb* themselves instead of working through the pain they're in. Although parents understood, I hope the Evil Queen warns my young readers about the dangers of bottling up their emotions.

EZMIA THE ENCHANTRESS

There's an evil enchantress inside all of us, especially when we're heartbroken. I mean, who wouldn't want to imprison the souls of their exes and display them inside jars across their mantel? No? Yeah, me neither...

As many people know, I started my career as an actor on a popular television show. It was an incredibly rewarding experience, but boy, I certainly learned where the phrase *It's lonely at the top* comes from. Jealousy ran thicker than water, and it was almost impossible to find someone trustworthy (the fact that I looked like the Pillsbury Doughboy also didn't help my love life). The heartbreak Ezmia experienced as a prolific fairy in the Fairy Kingdom is based on my own experiences of pursuing a personal life in the public eye.

Instead of becoming bitter and jaded from your own heartbreak, I *highly* recommend writing about a character who imprisons souls in jars and covers kingdoms in thorn-bush. It was the *exact* therapy I needed.

GENERAL JACQUES DU MARQUIS

There are thousands of incredible people in the entertainment industry, but it shouldn't shock anyone to know that there are some bad apples, too. General Marquis was inspired by a number of people I've encountered who are so addicted to notoricty, power, and money they've lost the ability to *enjoy* life. They're driven not by ambition but by something they're deeply ashamed of and desperate to hide. To them, success is the ultimate *shield* rather than an achievement. These are crippling and tragic qualities to have, but they're the perfect traits for a literary villain.

THE MASKED MAN/
LLOYD BAILEY

It was three AM on a Sunday in November 2012 and I was finishing up chapter twenty-nine of *The Enchantress Returns*. I was writing about Charlotte and Dr. Bob's wedding at the Charming Palace when a little voice popped into my mind and said, *The twins' father should come back from the dead and interrupt the vows.* I was so tempted by the idea that it paralyzed me; I stared at my computer screen for over an hour as I considered adding the twist. Ultimately, I hadn't decided whether or not I was going to even write a third Land of Stories book yet. I couldn't leave readers with such a traumatic cliffhanger if I wasn't *certain* there would be a sequel to follow it. So I promised myself I would make John Bailey's resurrection the ending of the third book if I continued the series.

In retrospect, it was a good decision. When the twins were separated at the end of book two, I received thousands of letters from distraught schoolchildren who couldn't handle the separation. I can't imagine how my readers would have reacted if the first Land of Stories cliffhanger involved the twins' father coming back to life—*however misleading it was.* In preparation for the wonderfully terrible hook, I started brainstorming the best way to present it in the story. I always knew it would end up being the twins' evil uncle, but I still needed to figure out the smartest way to introduce him.

One of my favorite unsolved mysteries is the story about the man in the iron mask, who was thought to be the brother of King Louis XIV of France (and the rightful heir to the French throne). The story had supplied me with hours of speculation over the years, and I knew the imagery would be a wonderful addition to the Land of Stories.

MORINA

When I started writing the Land of Stories in elementary school, I had intended for the Evil Queen and the Enchantress to team up in the plot of *The Wishing Spell*. At the time, I hadn't come up with the Evil Queen's backstory, or her history with the Enchantress, so they were simply two villains with the same priority: *destroy the fairy-tale world*!

I hadn't decided to call her the Enchantress or Ezmia until much later, so she was simply known as the thirteenth fairy (as the character is known in the Brothers Grimm version of "Sleeping Beauty"). The image of the thirteenth fairy was very different from what the Enchantress became—instead of hair that floated like fire in slow motion above her head and extra-long eyelashes, the character originally had horns on the sides of her face and wore a dress made of crow feathers. Looking back, I can see this was no doubt inspired by Disney's Maleficent, so I changed the character's look and her name to Ezmia. However, I came across my sketches of the thirteenth fairy while I was outlining *Beyond the Kingdoms* and was urged to include her somewhere in the series.

When you're writing *book four* of a series that you never intended to be longer than *one book*, you start looking for plot points to elaborate. Since everyone who reads the series falls in love with Froggy, I decided to tell the story about the witch who turned him into a frog. The cursed Charming prince's story is about self-acceptance, so I knew the witch had to relate to that somehow. At the time, I was filming *Glee* at Paramount Studios and drove past a plastic surgeon's office on my way to work— and the idea of Morina the beauty witch came to me. I loved the idea of a villain who altered her own appearance and the appearance of others with magic potions made from the youth of kidnapped children—*so deliciously evil*! Morina's shop is inspired by a beauty clinic in Los Angeles where I had a facial once, and those three customers we meet in *Beyond the Kingdoms* (the brunette, the redhead, and the blonde) are based on three women I saw at the clinic getting Botox injections.

IN CONCLUSION

I t's amazing what you learn about yourself when you're an author. Writing about the heroes of the Land of Stories has taught me what a *hero* truly is, and that affects my day-to-day choices. On the other hand, writing about the villains in the Land of Stories has taught me that I'm only three mistakes away from becoming one and how to prevent it.

I'm always asked, "What inspires you to write?" Well, after writing "Secrets from the Land of Stories," I'd say there's nothing that *doesn't* inspire me. If you have aspirations of becoming a writer, I think it's extremely important to keep your eyes open at all times. You never know when the hero or villain of your next story is going to pass you on the street.

BEHIND *the* SCENES: *the* ART *of the* LAND *of* STORIES

Chris's drawing from
childhood that started it all!

I drew this picture when I was in either the second or third grade at Mickey Cox Elementary School in Clovis, California. I remember I didn't have enough time to finish it in class, so I took it home and completed it over the weekend. At the time, I was really into *Teenage Mutant Ninja Turtles*, so I gave Goldilocks *sai* swords—but other than *that*, you can see very few changes have been made from the original plot I thought up as a child. This picture has always been on display wherever I've lived. Today it hangs in my office next to some of my favorite fan art from Land of Stories readers.

Brandon Dorman's initial cover sketch for
The Wishing Spell.

The revised sketch for
The Wishing Spell.

The final sketch.

The final cover!

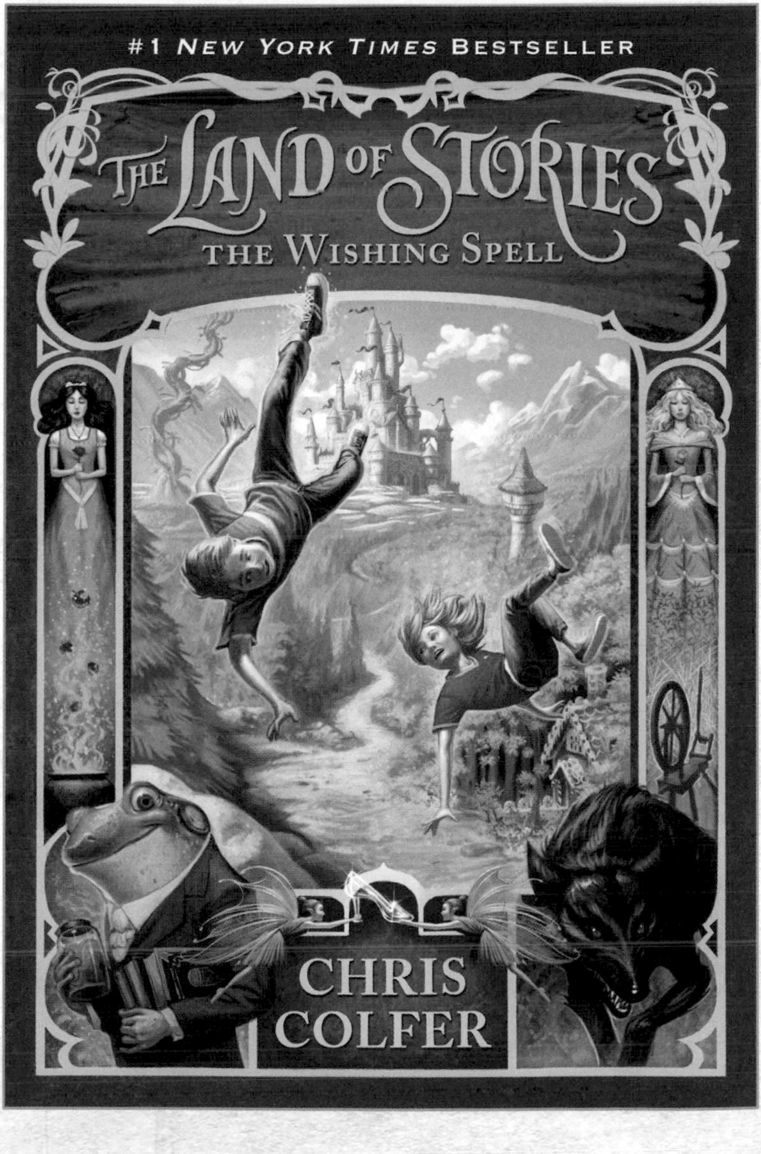

#1 NEW YORK TIMES BESTSELLER

THE LAND OF STORIES

THE WISHING SPELL

CHRIS COLFER

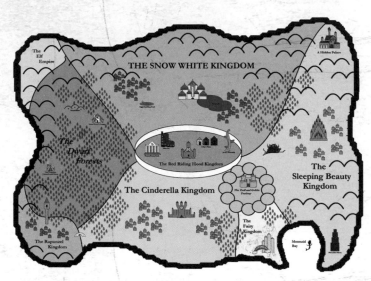

The map of the Land of Stories
that Chris created as a teenager.

Brandon's sketch of the first Land of Stories map.

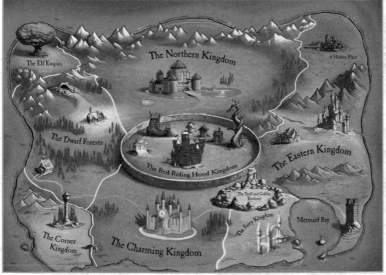

The gatefold maps in *The Wishing Spell* (top)
and *The Enchantress Returns* (bottom).
Can you spot the differences?

A few of Chris's chapter-header sketches for
The Wishing Spell.

Chapter Eight

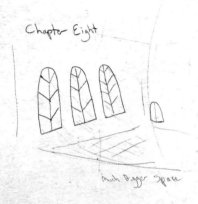

much bigger space

Chapter Eleven

more Camelot
than Viking

Chapter Eighteen

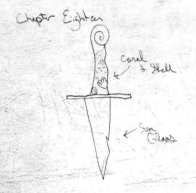

Coral & Shell

Sea Glass

Chapter Twenty-One

Magic Mirror

Brandon's final art.

Starting with book two, Chris supplied a cover sketch for Brandon to use as a guide. Here is Chris's sketch for *The Enchantress Returns.*

Brandon's final art!

THE *NEW YORK TIMES* BESTSELLER

THE LAND OF STORIES
THE ENCHANTRESS RETURNS

CHRIS COLFER

Chris's cover sketch for
A Grimm Warning.

Brandon's final art.

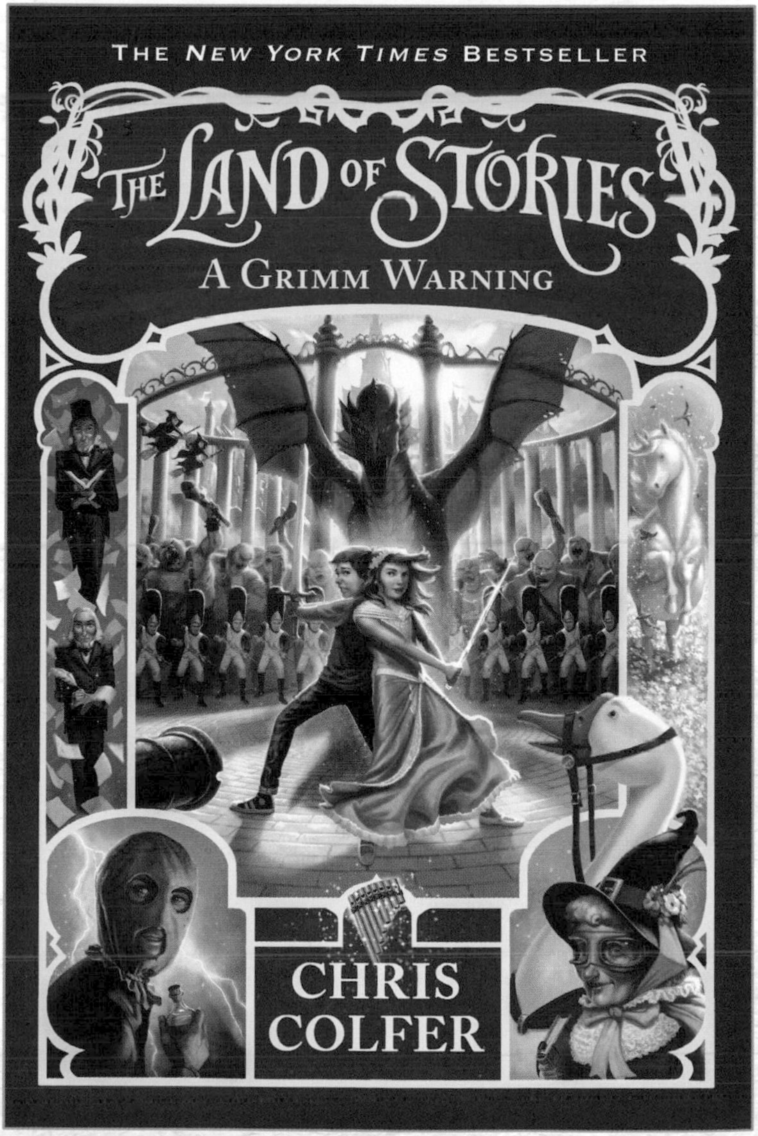

THE *NEW YORK TIMES* BESTSELLER

THE LAND OF STORIES

A GRIMM WARNING

CHRIS COLFER

Chris's cover sketch for
Beyond the Kingdoms.

Brandon's final art.

THE #1 *NEW YORK TIMES* BESTSELLING SERIES

THE LAND OF STORIES

BEYOND THE KINGDOMS

CHRIS COLFER

Chris's sketches and notes for the gatefold in
Beyond the Kingdoms.

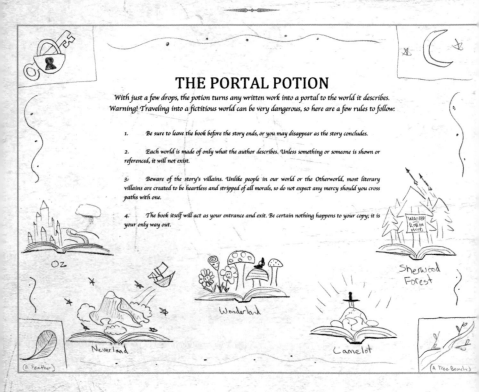

THE PORTAL POTION

With just a few drops, the potion turns any written work into a portal to the world it describes. Warning! Traveling into a fictitious world can be very dangerous, so here are a few rules to follow:

1. Be sure to leave the book before the story ends, or you may disappear as the story concludes.

2. Each world is made of only what the author describes. Unless something or someone is shown or referenced, it will not exist.

3. Beware of the story's villains. Unlike people in our world or the Otherworld, most literary villains are created to be heartless and stripped of all morals, so do not expect any mercy should you cross paths with one.

4. The book itself will act as your entrance and exit. Be certain nothing happens to your copy; it is your only way out.

Oz

Neverland

Wonderland

Camelot

Sherwood Forest

(A Feather)

(A Tree Branch)

Brandon's final gatefold art.

SHERWOOD FOREST

THE LAND OF OZ

CAMELOT

The Portal Potion

With just a few drops, the potion turns any written work into a portal to the world it describes. Now, I must warn about the dangers of entering a fictional world:

1. Time only exists as long as the story continues. Be sure to leave the book before the story ends, or you may disappear as the story concludes.
2. Each world is made of only what the author describes. Do not expect the characters to have any knowledge of our world or the Otherworld.
3. Beware of the story's villains. Unlike people in our world or the Otherworld, most literary villains are created to be heartless and stripped of all morals, so do not expect any mercy should you cross paths with one.
4. The book you choose to enter will act as your entrance and exit. Be certain nothing happens to it: it is your only way out.

WONDERLAND

NEVERLAND

Chris's cover sketch for
An Author's Odyssey.

Brandon's final art.

THE #1 *NEW YORK TIMES* BESTSELLING SERIES

THE LAND OF STORIES

AN AUTHOR'S ODYSSEY

CHRIS COLFER

Chris's cover sketch for
Worlds Collide.

Brandon's final art.

THE #1 *NEW YORK TIMES* BESTSELLING SERIES

THE LAND OF STORIES

WORLDS COLLIDE

CHRIS COLFER

More of Chris's character sketches!

An Elf

Coral

Elvina

Emerelda

Violetta

Xanthous

Mirror!

Mirror?

On the

Wall...

Trollbella

Esme

"Dave!"

Queen
Trollbella

Rosette

Skylene

Tangerina

FAN

ART

Alena P.

Alyssa M., Shoemakersville, Pennsylvania

Alyssa M., Columbus, Ohio

Fairy Council

Angela L., West Babylon, New York

Brooke L., Valley Village, California

Carter M., Indianapolis, Indiana

Chloe W., Louisville, Kentucky

Claire P., Dublin, California

Collin M., Oceanport, New Jersey

Denise H., Renton, Washington

Diana D., Rensselaer, New York

Holly S., Everett, Washington

Jennifer C., San Francisco, California

Jessica G., New York, New York

Lacey R., Victoria, Texas

Lennox G., Valley Village, California

Priya B., Poulsbo, Washington

Tasia G., Valencia, California

Taylor G., Tucson, Arizona

Zoë N., Atlanta, Georgia

Breanna B., Cranberry Township, Pennsylvania

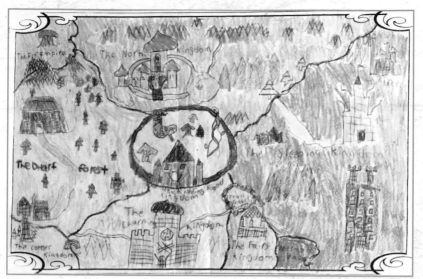

Jillian R., Fort Collins, Colorado

Savanna H., Rye, New York

Colin L., Seattle, Washington

from

CHRIS'S

DESK

During my senior year of high school, as a final for my Speech and Debate/Forensics class, we were assigned to teach an original lesson to our classmates. My lesson was "The Importance of Fairy Tales," and I basically gave the same lecture that Mrs. Peters gives her

students in chapter one of *The Wishing Spell*. As you can see, I transformed the classroom into the Land of Stories using butcher paper and lots and lots of duct tape. (This was not a requirement, but I've always been an overachiever.)

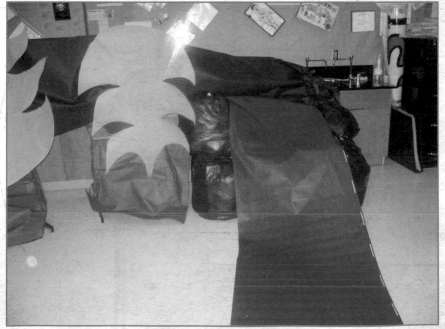

Even as a kindergartner, I had a thing for Mother Goose. I grew up near Fresno, California, and we were lucky enough to have a fairy-tale theme park called Storyland in the area. The park was a huge inspiration for the series and made the fairy-tale world seem so tangible to me.

I was seven years old when I started writing about the Bailey twins, and one of the most difficult parts was *naming* their adventures. *Storyland* was obviously taken, so after weeks of agonizing consideration, I decided to name Alex and Conner's escapades *the Land of Stories*. And the rest is history....

TLOS4: The Battle for Happily Ever After

✳ Prologue → FG meets with HCA. Gets idea for potion. Sees in Hall of Dreams her own son wants it to use it to take over the FTW.

✳ Book One → They try to track down MM. MM finds out witches prophecy meant something else. His team attacks RRK and steals four books: Alice, Peter Pan, Oz, & Princess & Goblin. Alex discovers FG kept a diary and realizes MM is their uncle & Emmerich is their cousin. *Owl guides her. _(MM tells them they have to get more men)_

✳ Book Two → Bree is having a hard time coping. She and Emmerich are pen-pals. Emmerich's mom tells him the truth. Bree figures out she's the descendant of Wilhelm Grimm. Emmerich gets kidnapped, Bree finds a way into the Land of Stories. _(• He looks into Family history too)_

✳ Book Three → The heroes go into first book "Peter Pan" searching for MM & Emmerich. Alex & Conner are led to recruit Pirates are gone — they were recruited. They learn a little bit about the relationship.

✳ Book Four → They travel into Oz. They meet up with the tin man. (• Peter who tells them the Wicked Witch of the West hasn't been seen in a very long time. The twins realized an army is being formed. _(follows them)_

✳ Book Five → Wonderland. The twins don't find Emmerich in there either. They know they're gonna real bad up.

Originally, _Beyond the Kingdoms, An Author's Odyssey,_ and _Worlds Collide_ were going to be one big book called _The Land of Stories: The Battle for Happily Ever After._ These are my notes outlin-

*Book Six → The twins and the gang go into Camelot to recruit the Knights of the Round Table. MG has a flirtation with Merlin.

*Book Seven → The Notebook. They decide to bargain with the MM before someone gets hurt. Carmen's notebook is full of crazy places to fight. The last story is Bree's → Cemetery off the Undead. All famously killed warriors come back to life.

*Book Eight → ~~IX~~ Happily/Ever After ~~the End~~
• Everyone goes their separate ways.
• They visit their Dad.

Epilogue → Crazy Grandpa Bailey tells grandchildren his stories. His own kids used to believe it - now they want him to go to a home... Alex magically meets up with him. Maybe Grandma Bree doesn't remember her epic life? They leave the storybook behind.

ing the gargantuan plot. Shortly afterward, I realized there was just too much story for one book and decided to split it into three separate installments. It was one of the best decisions I've ever made.

This is my very first draft of the last paragraph of the series. It was one of the most important paragraphs I've ever had to write and took me over three hours to finalize.

As Alex and Conner watched the sun set over the Land of Stories, they each sighed with the biggest relief of their young lives. They knew there would be challenges ahead, they knew there would be unseen dangers in the days to come, they knew their period of piece would eventually be interupted—

However, for the first time Alex and Conner didn't fear what they

Couldn't see, because no matter what dilemma they crossed paths with, they knew it'd be nothing they couldn't handle. And because of that, the Bailey twins had finally learned how to have a _happily ever after_, after all.

TLOS6 WORD/PAGE COUNT

P - Ch. 5	82 pages	20,786
ch 6 - 13	88 pages	22,010
ch. 14 - 19	98 pages	23,925
20	9	2,166 2,144 2,214
21	13	3,332 3,375
22	8	2009
23	7	1594
24	10	2395
25	8	2181

TLOS1 — 438
TLOS2 — 517
3 — 469
4 — 419
5 — 438
6 —

$24 \overline{)323}$
80,319
188 = 506.65
1.6 = 516.8
5x100 = 400

$22 \overline{)293}$
74,228
x1.55 — 461.9
x1.6 — 462.4

$011 \overline{)290}$ / 72,214
x1.55 — 449.5
x1.6 — 464
5x1000 — 360

P - 19 = 66,721 / 265
5x1000 — 333.5 g5s

1.55 = 415.4
1.6 = 428.8

I t was a goal of mine to make each Land of Stories book roughly the same length. The best way I kept track of length was by recording each chapter's word count. Usually, the way the series is formatted, a thousand words equal five pages. It was a pretty tedious exercise and almost always required a calculator.

These are my notes outlining all the battle sequences in New York City toward the end of *Worlds Collide*. I wanted to incorporate as many famous landmarks as possible and took three different trips to the Big Apple to help me narrow down my list. To date, I have never written anything more action-packed than the final chapters of *Worlds Collide*. By the time I was finished, I was more exhausted than the characters who were actually in the battle.

(I)

- Charlotte & Bob are keeping books when Arnette & Froggy arrive.
    - Arthur tells Charlotte who he is
        - We need to talk!
                                                        (Ellis Island)
- Froggy leads FC to Central Park.
- Arthur takes charge of Literary Army. (Talks to classic Authors?)

- Witches versus the Fairies.
    - Alex gets distracted → shield goes up   (Central Park)
    - Sniper tries to take out Alex, Beadle jumps in front.
        - Alex goes berzerk, heads to Freedom Tower
        - Morina runs after Alex.
        - Remaining Witches flee — take Hero with them.

Jolly Roger vs. Dalay Llama
    - Peter Pan defeats Captain Hook (Empire State Building)

Flying Monkeys vs. Zemons   (Chrysler Building)
    - Blubbo talks to parents, steals Witches Cap
    - Lost Boys throw water balloons at W.W

Card Soldiers vs. Cyborg Army   (Union Square)
    - Queen of Hearts cuts Cyborg Queens head off.
    - Arthur & Tinwoodman & Tinkerbell pops out of Tin Woodmans chest.

- Winkies vs. Mummy   (Air)   ②
  - Conor, Dmc, Jack, Goldilocks find Engre & Bear
- Witch Hunt
  - They hop from Dream to Dream to Save Hero.
  - They all regroup

- Everyone ~~regroups~~ on the Statue of Liberty.
- Alex ~~begins~~ to Cover NYC in vines

- Marion vs. Fairy Council   (Times Square)
  - Marion. makes Alex really upset, vines start growing,
    lightning starts.
- Marion fights off fairies → Red & Froggy handle them
  - Alex flies to Freedom Tower   • Then get married — their Conor & others show up

---

- Everyone regroups.   (Statue of Liberty)
- Alex starts covering all NYC in vines & lightning
- Conor comes up with plan. "How many of me can you put on your body?"
- 4 Conors trick Alex (Conor, Jack, Robin Arthur)   (Freedom Tower)
- They /go inside Short Storey

- Alex & Conor have moment with their Dad.   (Story)   ③
  - They get out before story crumbles
- Alex is back to normal   (NYC)
- They "heal city" with Hazelton's Fire
- Say Goodbye to all characters
- Alex has an idea

Presidet wakes up from dream   (White House)
- Alex & Conor tell her the worlds been asleep.

- Fairies rebuild incredible Fairy Palace.
- Mother Goose looks into crystal ball — Alex & Arthur will be   (Fairy Kingdom)
                                     together in the end.
- Alex & Conor on balcony
      ↳ Happily Ever After

Epilogue

<u>Quotes</u>

• "You can't out-smart someone logic doesn't apply to!" - Red

• "You know, they modeled Lady Liberty after me." -Mother Goose

• "~~Where else would it want~~ I couldn't think of a better
   place to get married, than the ashes of your nex-girlfriend."
   -Red.

• "Times Square"

• "Who is this Hamilton fellow? Any relation to Shakespeare's Hamlet?"
   -Red

S ometimes great character quotes will hit me before I
even know where I'm going to put them in the book.
I knew Red and Froggy were going to get married in
Worlds Collide after they defeated Morina, and I knew I
wanted Red to say something ridiculous about it, but it
took me a few days to figure out what. Then one night,
Red's voice popped into my head and said, "I can't think
of a better place to get married than on the ashes of your
ex-girlfriend." It was so *perfectly* Red that I had to get up
and walk away from my desk.

This was a very early outline for the beginning of *Worlds Collide*. As you can see, the original order was very different from what made it into the book. I think making outlines is important, but I always stray from them once I start writing. Sometimes chapters feel completely different after you finish them and you decide in the moment that *another* part of the story should follow them.

TLOS 6...

- Conner as an old man. Can't remember what happened to Alex.
  - Books included:
    - Fairytelotopia
    - Starboardia
    - Galaxy Queen
    - Blimp Bay
    - The Great New York Adventure
  - He can't remember so he turns to "The Great New York Adventure."

> "The best fiction is truth in disguise."

- The Hospital, no one knows where Alex went.
  - The News gives a clue. — Something is happening in NYC.

- A maid working at the Palace Hotel saw a portal. Rusty Bagraswin saw the same thing at Belvedere Palace A New York City Cop saw something too.

- Alex visits Arthur → Marina can control her. "You and what Army?"

- Witches emerge from Public Library, go to Central Park, take it over.

- Conner and friends use abandoned Subway to move around NYC.

The first letter is a large decorative "T".

here are hundreds and hundreds of characters in the Land of Stories, and although they're all crucial to the series, I'm guilty of forgetting one or two from time to time. These are lists I made after writing *An Author's Odyssey* of all the characters whose arcs I had to tie up in *Worlds Collide* and all the different dimensions they're from. Even with all these listed, I'm sure some Book Huggers out there will spot a few names missing and let me know about it.

Otherworld
- Alex
- Conner
- Charlotte
- Bob
- Bree
- Emmerich
- Cornelia
- Warden
- Freda
- Wendy
- Mark
- Linda
- Cindy
- President
- Gerald?
- John Bailey
- South Bank Lion

TLOS
- Red
- Froggy
- Jack
- Goldilocks
- Trollbella
- Emerelda
- Xanthous
- Skylene
- Tangerina
- Rosette
- Violetta
- Coral
- Hagetta
- Traveling Tradesman
- Rook
- Froggbo Robins
- Cinderella
- Snow White
- Sleeping Beauty
- Rapunzel
- Queen
- Chase
- Clawdius
- Clawdilla
- Lester
- Mother Goose
- Hero
- Clawdina
- Evly

- Morina
- Rat-Mary
- Clawentine
- Trondissima
- Serpentina
- Sea Witch
- Snow Queen
- Arboris
- Wildero
- Trix
- Noelle
- Cornelius
- Merble
- George Clamy
- Princess Hope
- Princess Ash
- Lampton
- Sir Grant
- Porridge
- Bootie
- Oats
- Bones
- Red's Granny
- Little Old Woman

O2
- Tin Woodman
- Bluebo
- Wicked Witch
- Winkies
- Flying Monkeys

Wonderland
- Queen of Hearts
- Card Soldiers

Neverland
- Peter Pan
- Tinkerbell
- Captain Hook
- Schme
- Tootles
- Slightly
- Curley
- Lost Twins
- Jolly Roger Pirates
- Nibs

Camelot
- Arthur
- Merlin
- ~~Knights of the Round Table~~

Sherwood Forest
- Robin Hood
- Friar Tuck
- Little John
- Will Scarlet
- Alan-a-Dale

TLOSS — 97,172

30,000
× ?
90,000

GG Armies
- Merry Men / Lost Boys
- Knights of Camelot
- Starboardia Pirates
- The Zemons
- Mummy Army
- Cyborg Army

Starboardia

- Auburn Sally
- Raggy Charter
- Admiral Swordman
- Navy Men
- Whirling Wooly
- Fish Lips Lucy
- Somersault Sydney
- Porcelain-Face Patty
- Stinky-Foot Phoebe
- Peg-Legged Peggy
- High-Tide Tabitha
- Catfish Kate
- Too-Much-Rum Amber
- Dig-Booty Bertha
- Not-So-Jolly Joan
- Siren Sue

The Zeroes

- Bolt
- Whipray
- Morph
- Blaze
- Professor-Willet

Other

- Medusa

Gaalaxy Queen

- Cyborg Queen
- Neutrino
- Cyborg Army
- Bliss Worm

Blimp Boy

- Smyge
- Beau Rogers
- Mummy Army
- Bones

One of the greatest privileges of writing the Land of Stories was getting to travel the world for research. From the fields of Central Park in New York City to the halls of Neuschwanstein Castle in Germany, I've covered a lot of ground in hopes of authentically describing all the locations in the series. Many of the thoughts and emotions the characters feel while exploring the various landmarks were the exact feelings I had while experiencing them.

The gravesite of the Brothers Grimm in Berlin,
Germany. I was pleasantly surprised by all the flowers
and notes of gratitude people still leave today.

A spectacular view of Neuschwanstein Castle from
the Marienbrücke (Queen Mary's Bridge) in
Schwangau, Germany. Seeing the castle with my
own eyes convinced me that the fairy-tale world
isn't as far away as we think.

The South Bank Lion watching over the River Thames in London, England. Whenever I'm in London, no matter how busy I am, I always make time to visit the statue so he doesn't worry about me.

An impressive stairwell in the New York Public
Library's main branch. I feel slightly guilty for
blowing up the library in *Worlds Collide*.

The One World Observatory at One World
Trade Center in New York City. I tried to get on the
roof to research the finale of *Worlds Collide*,
but this was as close as I could get.

CHRIS'S TOP TEN TIPS *for* WRITERS (*Which He's* STILL *Learning*)

START!

As obvious as it sounds, the most common problem I hear from aspiring writers is the difficulty in *starting* a writing project. I completely understand their hesitation; writing is a much bigger commitment than people realize. Similar to when you adopt a pet, if you don't give your idea the proper attention, affection, and nourishment, it might run away and die. Before you begin, make sure you're in the right headspace, find a peaceful environment, and give yourself plenty of time to work.

With that said, sometimes people romanticize what writing is, and their expectations prevent them from starting. Prior to the Land of Stories, whenever I visualized the act of writing, I always imagined J. K. Rowling putting quill to paper in a remote castle overlooking a spacious Scottish estate. Currently as I write this, I am in my Star Wars/Marvel–themed guest room, dressed in Grumpy Cat pajamas, and looking at dozens of half-empty Diet Coke cans scattered across my desk. While it's important to be relaxed, if you're waiting for the *perfect* moment and the *perfect* place to appear before you begin writing, you'll probably be waiting a *very* long time.

⊷⊙ 2 ⊙⊶
WORD VOMIT

Writers tend to be perfectionists. We expect every sentence to flow perfectly from our minds to the page with little or no correction needed, but nothing is going to sound perfect the first time you write it—that's why God invented rough drafts. You'll do yourself a favor if you allow imperfection in the beginning stages. For example, I came back to this paragraph seven different times before I was happy enough to move on.

At first, just spit everything out that you want to say—don't worry if it sounds pretty or if it's even legible. Once you have the basic idea of what you're working toward, go back and edit it until you're content.

⊷⊙ 3 ⊙⊶
COMPLETE SATISFACTION IS A MYTH

While it's important to be proud of your work, I've never met a writer who has experienced complete, over-the-moon satisfaction with something they've written. We'll always look at our own work and want to fix things here and there. That's the beauty and frustration of writing—it's never truly finished!

Give yourself enough time to properly edit it, but don't torture yourself over every other word. A good stopping place is when you're no longer *improving* something and just *changing* it. Remember, just because something is different doesn't make it better.

GIVE YOURSELF
A DEADLINE

A deadline is a great motivator, but it doesn't have to come from an editor or a publisher. If you need an extra boost to get something done, make a deadline with a friend or family member you can trust with your writing. Not only will this help you finish your work, it'll also get you used to having your work read by other people.

5
DON'T BE INTIMIDATED

Unfortunately, the world is full of people who criticize for sport. It's easier said than done, but you cannot let anyone intimidate you to the point of giving up. There will always be people who are smarter and better writers than you—but what if your story is better than theirs? While experience and education help you become a better storyteller, it doesn't always help with creativity. Sometimes being a good writer has nothing to do with style or skill, but depends solely on your imagination. Remember, if you have a story in your heart, then you have the right to write it.

6
IMMERSE, IMMERSE, IMMERSE

When you're writing, it's easy to become a total recluse and lock yourself away from sunlight and all civilization. (There was a period when I didn't leave my house for three weeks!) As easy as it is to disappear, to stay creative it's crucial to get fresh air and immerse yourself in anything you possibly can. Read as many books as you can, watch as many new movies and television shows as you can handle, go to museums and look at artwork, take hikes and walks through areas you've never been before, listen to music you normally wouldn't listen to. The more you stimulate your creativity muscles, the better your writing will become.

— 7 —
HOW TO DEAL WITH WRITER'S BLOCK

Writer's block is a vicious and taxing cycle. The more you suffer from it, the stronger it becomes. That's why my best advice for writer's block is to get up and do something else the moment you feel it coming on. Do a puzzle, walk your dog, ride your bike—whatever you can do to take your mind off it. Give your imagination a chance to rejuvenate itself before attempting to pick up the pen again. It's always when I force myself to relax that an idea will hit me and reinvigorate my patience and creativity. It's kind of rude now that I think about it.

8

WRITE WHAT YOU KNOW

Every writer has had their fair share of unique experiences and encounters—try incorporating as much of yourself into your writing as possible. Even though the Land of Stories is about people and creatures in a magical dimension, each character and situation is based on someone or something I know very well. Writing from a place of familiarity adds a wonderful element of truth to your work and makes the process much more fun.

9

SUBSTANCE OVER STYLE

In the beginning, too many writers make the mistake of valuing *how* they're writing over *what* they're writing. As much as we all want to write as suspensefully as Stephen King or as lyrically as William Shakespeare, I believe it's better to develop your own style over time than to start off by copying another author's style. Even if it's flawed at first, originality will capture someone's attention more than a bad impression.

10

DON'T FORGET
TO ENJOY IT

B y the time you gain the concentration needed to start something, tell the story in the style you want, meet a crushing deadline, and build up the courage to share your work with someone else—you may be so emotionally and physically exhausted, you've forgotten why you enjoy writing at all. Upon completion, it's important to take a step back and be proud of yourself. Even if your hard work doesn't amount to anything, you've still accomplished what most people have only dreamed of.

A quote from the Fairy Godmother always reminds me of why I love writing so much: "Creativity is the simple but powerful ability to make something from nothing, and it just so happens that *making something from nothing* is also the definition of *magic.*"

CONCLUSION

I wish I could go back in time and tell my eight-year-old self about everything the Land of Stories has become. Without a doubt, I would find him staying up late on a Saturday night, eating a box of chocolate doughnuts, and struggling to write about the Bailey twins with his limited vocabulary. His chubby cheeks would probably explode if he heard he was a future #1 internationally bestselling author and that his Land of Stories would expand to over a dozen books. Granted, he would be upset that it took twenty years to happen, but *patience* has never been my strong suit.

I remember the day the Land of Stories first came to me like it was yesterday. I was about six years old and had been in the hospital for three weeks due to complications after an operation. These were the dark ages before iPads, so my mom brought me a stack of books from home to keep me entertained. Among them was an old treasury of fairy tales she used to read to me every night before bed. As I flipped through the pages, I remember desperately hoping the book would to come to life and pull me into the fairy-tale world so I could escape my hospital bed. I visualized all the places I wanted to see, all the characters I wanted to meet, and all the adventures I wanted to have with them. Remarkably, 90 percent of *The Wishing Spell*'s plot was invented while I was waiting to be released from the hospital.

Having my own world to escape into came in handy a few years later. My younger sister was diagnosed with a very rare and serious form of epilepsy. It was an incredibly difficult and scary time for my family. We flew all over the country to meet with doctors and specialists, only to return empty-handed after every appointment. My parents had to work overtime to pay for medical bills and I was left to myself a lot, but luckily I had the Land of Stories to keep me occupied. The more I daydreamed about it, the clearer it became, and soon my little mental vacations turned into an obsession.

Every day after school, I would race home and use my mom's computer to type out whatever I had dreamed up that day (while I should have been paying attention in class). Once I finished a two- to three-page "chapter," I'd ride my bike to my grandmother's house and have her edit it for me. If my grandmother liked a chapter, she would keep it in a pile with the others, but if she thought I could do better, she would crumple it up and send me back home to rewrite it.

"Grandma, I'm never going to be a good writer!" I moaned on one occasion. "It's just too hard."

"Christopher, wait until you're done with elementary school before you worry about being a failed writer," she replied.

Looking back, I now understand just how lucky I was to have someone like my grandmother in my corner. By believing in me, she taught me to believe in myself and gave me all the tools I needed to make it happen. Even though she knew my writing needed a lot of work, and even though she knew the publishing world was very difficult to break into, it never stopped her from encouraging me and lifting me up when I needed a helping hand.

So if there are any kiddos out there reading this who have their own universe stuck in their head but no one to champion it, please allow me to be that champion for you. Don't ever think you don't have what it takes to make your literary dreams a reality. Now more than ever, we need stories from people of all different types and backgrounds and from all corners of the world to inspire, encourage, and shape a better future. So please, put aside your pessimism and pick up a pen—you might have *exactly* what the world needs! Even if you don't believe it at first, always remember that sometimes the universe has bigger plans for us than we have for ourselves.

While the future holds many exciting possibilities for the Land of Stories universe—*prequels and sequels and films, oh my!*—I've learned that we should *never* take the present for granted. So, from the bottom of my heart, I want to thank every one of my readers for going on these adventures with me. It has been the greatest privilege of my life to tell you stories about the big, crazy, and magical world that's existed inside of me for as long as I can remember. No matter what happens in the days to come, I hope the Land of Stories will continue to be as wonderful an escape for you as it has been for me.

Until the next
adventure,

Chris

XO

ACKNOWLEDGMENTS

I'd like to thank everyone on my amazing team, especially Rob Weisbach, Derek Kroeger, Alla Plotkin, Rachel Karten, Heather Manzutto, Marcus Colen, ICM, and ID-PR.

The wonderful people at Little, Brown, including Alvina Ling, Megan Tingley, Nikki Garcia, Jessica Shoffel, Carol Scatorchio, Jackie Engel, Kristin Delaney, Svetlana Keselman, Emilie Polster, Janelle DeLuise, Bethany Strout, Jen Graham, Sasha Illingworth, and Virginia Lawther.

Jerry Maybrook for producing all the audiobooks in the Land of Stories series.

The insanely talented Brandon Dorman for bringing my imaginary best friends to life.

My friends and family for loving me—quirks and all!

And most importantly, all the incredible Book Huggers from around the world. Thanks for making this guide possible!

Turn the page for a preview of

AVAILABLE NOW!

AN UNEXPECTED AUDIENCE

Magic was outlawed in all four kingdoms—
and that was putting it lightly. Legally,
magic was the worst criminal act a person
could commit, and socially, there was nothing considered more despicable. In most areas, just being *associ-
ated* with a convicted witch or warlock was an offense
punishable by death.

In the Northern Kingdom, perpetrators and their
families were put on trial and promptly burned at the
stake. In the Eastern Kingdom, very little evidence

was needed to sentence the accused and their loved ones to hang at the gallows. And in the Western Kingdom, suspected witches and warlocks were drowned without any trial whatsoever.

The executions were rarely committed by law enforcement or kingdom officials. Most commonly, the punishments were carried out by mobs of angry citizens who took the law into their own hands. Although frowned upon, the brutal sport was completely tolerated by the kingdoms' sovereigns. In truth, the leaders were delighted their people had something besides government to direct their anger toward. So the monarchs welcomed the distraction and even encouraged it during times of political unrest.

"He or she who chooses a path of magic has chosen a path of condemnation," King Nobleton of the North proclaimed. Meanwhile, *his* negligent choices were causing the worst famine in his kingdom's history.

"We must never show sympathy to people with such abominable priorities," Queen Endustria of the

East declared, and then immediately raised taxes to finance a summer palace.

"Magic is an insult to God and nature, and a danger to morality as we know it," King Warworth of the West remarked. Luckily for him, the statement distracted his people from rumors about the eight illegitimate children he had fathered with eight different mistresses.

Once a witch or warlock was exposed, persecution was nearly impossible to escape. Many fled into the thick and dangerous forest known as the In-Between that grew between borders. Unfortunately, the In-Between was home to dwarfs, elves, goblins, trolls, ogres, and all the other species humankind had banished over the years. The witches and warlocks seeking asylum in the woods usually found a quick and violent demise at the hands of a barbaric creature.

The only mercy whatsoever for witch-and-warlock-kind (if it could even be considered *mercy*) was found in the Southern Kingdom.

As soon as King Champion XIV inherited the

throne from his father, the late Champion XIII, his first royal decree was to abolish the death penalty for convicted practitioners of magic. Instead, the offenders were sentenced to life imprisonment with hard labor (and they were reminded every day how *grateful* they should be). The king didn't amend the law purely out of the goodness of his heart, but as an attempt to make peace with a traumatic memory.

When Champion was a child, his own mother was beheaded for a "suspected interest" in magic. The charge came from Champion XIII himself, so no one thought to question the accusation or investigate the queen's innocence, although Champion XIII's motives were questioned on the day following his wife's execution, when he married a much younger and prettier woman. Since the queen's untimely end, Champion XIV had counted down the days until he could avenge his mother by destroying his father's legacy. And as soon as the crown was placed on his head, Champion XIV devoted most of his reign to erasing Champion XIII from the Southern Kingdom's history.

Now in old age, King Champion XIV spent the majority of his time doing the least he possibly could. His royal decrees had been reduced to grunts and eye rolls. Instead of royal visitations, the king lazily waved to crowds from the safety of a speeding carriage. And the closest thing he made to royal statements anymore were complaints about his castle's halls being "too long" and the staircases "too steep."

Champion made a hobby of avoiding people—especially his self-righteous family. He ate his meals alone, went to bed early, slept in late, and cherished his lengthy afternoon naps (and God have mercy on the poor soul that woke him before he was ready).

Although on one particular afternoon, the king was prematurely woken, not by a careless grandchild or clumsy chambermaid, but by a sudden change in the weather. Champion awoke with fright to heavy raindrops thudding against his chamber windows and powerful winds whistling down his chimney. It had been such a sunny and clear day when he went to bed, so the storm was quite a surprise for the groggy sovereign.

"I've risen," Champion announced.

The king waited for the nearest servant to scurry in and help him down from his tall bed, but his call was unanswered.

Champion aggressively cleared his throat. "I said *I've risen*," he called again, but strangely, there was still no response.

The king's joints cracked as he begrudgingly climbed out of bed, and he mumbled a series of curse words as he hobbled across the stone floor to retrieve his robe and slippers. Once he was dressed, Champion burst through his chamber doors, intending to scold the first servant he laid eyes on.

"Why is no one responding? What could possibly be more important than—"

Champion fell silent and looked around in disbelief. The drawing room outside his chambers was usually bustling with maids and butlers, but now it was completely empty. Even the soldiers who guarded the doors day and night had abandoned their posts.

The king peered into the hallway beyond the

drawing room, but it was just as empty. Not only was it vacant of servants and soldiers, but all the *light* had disappeared, too. Every candle in the chandeliers and all the torches on the walls had been extinguished.

"Hello?" Champion called down the hall. "Is anyone there?" But all he heard was his own voice echoing back to him.

The king cautiously moved through the castle searching for another living soul, but he only found more and more darkness at every turn. It was incredibly unsettling—he had lived in the castle since he was a small boy and had never seen it so lifeless. Champion looked through every window he passed, but the rain and fog blocked his view of anything outside.

Eventually the king rounded the corner of a long hallway and spotted flickering lights coming from his private study. The door was wide open and someone was enjoying a fire inside. It would have been a very inviting sight if the circumstances weren't so eerie. With each step he took, the king's heart beat faster and faster, and he anxiously peered into the doorway to see who or what was waiting inside.

"Oh, look! The king is awake!"

"Finally."

"Now, now, girls. We must be respectful to His Majesty."

The king found two young girls and a beautiful woman sitting on the sofa in his study. Upon his entrance, they quickly rose from their seats and bowed in his direction.

"Your Majesty, what a pleasure to make your acquaintance," the woman said.

She wore an elegant purple gown that matched her large bright eyes, and curiously, only one glove, which covered her left arm. Her dark hair was tucked beneath an elaborate fascinator with flowers, feathers, and a short veil that fell over her face. The girls couldn't have been older than ten, and wore plain white robes and cloth headwraps.

"Who the heck are you?" Champion asked.

"Oh, forgive me," the woman said. "I'm Madame Weatherberry and these are my apprentices, Miss

Tangerina Turkin and Miss Skylene Lavenders. I hope you don't mind that we made ourselves at home in your study. We've traveled an awfully long way to be here and couldn't resist a nice fire while we waited."

Madame Weatherberry seemed to be a very warm and charismatic woman. She was the last person the king had expected to find in the abandoned castle, which in many ways made the woman *and* the situation even stranger. Madame Weatherberry extended her right arm to shake Champion's hand, but he didn't accept the friendly gesture. Instead, the monarch looked his unexpected guests up and down and took a full step backward.

The girls giggled and eyed the paranoid king, as if they were looking into his soul and found it laughable.

"This is a private room in a royal residence!" Champion reprimanded them. "How dare you enter without permission! I could have you whipped for this!"

"Please pardon our intrusion," Madame Weatherberry said. "It's rather out of character for us to barge into someone's home unannounced, but I'm afraid I had no choice. You see, I've been writing to your secretary, Mr. Fellows, for quite some time. I was hoping to schedule an audience with you, but unfortunately, Mr. Fellows never responded to any of my letters— he's a rather inefficient man, if you don't mind me saying it. Perhaps it's time to replace him? Anyway, there's a very timely matter I'm eager to discuss with you, so here we are."

"How did this woman get inside?" the king shouted into the empty castle. "Where in God's name is everyone?!"

"I'm afraid all your subjects are indisposed at the moment," Madame Weatherberry informed him.

"What do you mean *indisposed*?" Champion barked.

"Oh, it's nothing to be concerned about—*just a little enchantment to secure our safety*. I promise, all your servants and soldiers will return once we've had time to talk. I find diplomacy is so much easier when there are no distractions, don't you?"

Madame Weatherberry spoke in a calm manner, but one word made Champion's eyes grow wide and his blood pressure soar.

"*Enchantment?*" The king gasped. "You're… you're…*you're a WITCH!*"

Champion pointed his finger at Madame Weatherberry in such a panic he pulled every muscle in his right shoulder. The king groaned as he clutched his arm, and his guests snickered at his dramatic display.

"No, Your Majesty, I am not a *witch*," she said.

"Don't you lie to me, woman!" the king shouted. "Only witches make enchantments!"

"No, Your Majesty, that is not true."

"You're a witch and you've cursed this castle with magic! You'll pay for this!"

"I see listening isn't your strong suit," Madame Weatherberry said. "Perhaps if I repeated myself three times my message would sink in? I find that's a helpful tool with slow learners. Here we go—*I am not a witch. I am not a witch. I am not a—*"

"IF YOU'RE NOT A WITCH, THEN WHAT ARE YOU?"

It didn't matter how loud the king yelled or how agitated he became; Madame Weatherberry's polite demeanor never faded.

"Actually, Your Majesty, that's among the topics I would like to discuss with you this evening," she said. "Now, we don't wish to take any more of your time than necessary. Won't you please have a seat so we can begin?"

As if pulled by an invisible hand, the chair behind the king's desk moved on its own, and Madame Weatherberry gestured for him to sit. Champion wasn't certain he had a choice in the matter, so he took a seat and nervously glanced back and forth at the visitors. The girls sat on the sofa and folded their hands neatly in their laps. Madame Weatherberry sat between her apprentices and flipped her veil upward so she could look the sovereign directly in the eye.

"First, I wanted to thank you, Your Majesty," Madame Weatherberry began. "You're the only ruler in history to show the magical community any mercy—granted, some might say life imprisonment with hard labor is worse than death—but it's still a step in the right direction. And I'm confident we can turn these steps into strides if we just—Your Majesty, is something wrong? I don't seem to have your full attention."

Bizarre buzzing and swishing noises had captured the king's curiosity as she spoke. He looked around the study but couldn't find the source of the odd noises.

"Sorry, I thought I heard something," the king said. "You were saying?"

"I was professing my gratitude for the mercy you've shown the magical community."

The king grunted with disgust. "Well, you're mistaken if you think I have any empathy for the *magical community*," he scoffed. "On the contrary, I believe magic is just as foul and unnatural as all the other sovereigns do. My concern is with the people who use magic to take advantage of the law."

"And that's commendable, sir," Madame Weatherberry said. "Your devotion to justice is what separates you from all the other monarchs. Now, I'd like to enlighten your perspective on magic, so you may continue making this kingdom a fairer and safer place for *all* your people. After all, justice cannot exist for one if it doesn't exist for everyone."

Their conversation had just begun and the king was already starting to resent it. "What do you mean *enlighten* my perspective?" he sneered.

"Your Majesty, the way magic is criminalized and stigmatized is the greatest injustice of our time. But with the proper modifications and amendments— *and some strategic publicity*—we can change all that. Together, we can create a society that encourages all walks of life and raises them to their greatest potential and—Your Majesty, are you listening? I seem to have lost you again."

Once more, the king was distracted by the mysterious buzzing and swishing sounds. His eyes searched the study more frantically than before and he only heard every other word Madame Weatherberry said.

"I must have misunderstood you," he said. "For a moment, it sounded as if you were suggesting the *legalization of magic*."

"Oh, there was no misunderstanding," Madame Weatherberry said with a laugh. "The legalization of magic is *exactly* what I'm suggesting."

Champion suddenly sat up in his seat and clenched the armrests of his chair. Madame Weatherberry had his undivided attention now. She couldn't possibly be implying something so ludicrous.

"What is wrong with you, woman?" the king sneered. "Magic can *never* be legalized!"

"Actually, sir, it's very much in the realm of possibility," Madame Weatherberry said. "All that's required is a simple decree that decriminalizes the act and then, in good time, the stigma surrounding it will diminish."

"I would sooner decriminalize murder and thievery!" the king declared. "The Lord clearly states in the Book of Faith that magic is a horrendous sin, and therefore a *crime* in this kingdom! And if crimes didn't have consequences, we would live in utter chaos!"

"That's where you're mistaken, Your Majesty," she said. "You see, magic is *not* the crime the world thinks it is."

"*Of course it is!*" he objected. "I have witnessed magic being used to trick and torment innocent people! I have seen the bodies of children who were slaughtered for potions and spells! I have been to villages plagued by curses and hexes! So don't you dare defend magic to me, Madame! The magical community will never receive an ounce of sympathy or understanding from *this* sovereign!"

Champion couldn't have made his opposition any clearer, but Madame Weatherberry moved to the edge of her seat and smiled as if they had found common ground.

"This may surprise you, sir, but I completely agree," she said.

"You do?" he asked with a suspicious gaze.

"Oh yes, *completely*," she repeated. "I believe those who torment innocent people *should* be punished for their actions—*and harshly*, I might add. There's just one minor flaw in your reasoning. The situations you've witnessed aren't caused by magic but by *witchcraft*."

The king tensed his brow and glanced at Madame

Weatherberry as if she were speaking a foreign language. *"Witchcraft?"* he said mockingly. "I've never heard of such a thing."

"Then allow me to explain," Madame Weatherberry said. "Witchcraft is a ghastly and destructive practice. It stems from a dark desire to *deceive* and *disrupt.* Only people with wicked hearts are capable of witchcraft, and believe me, they deserve whatever fate they bring upon themselves. But *magic* is something else entirely. At its core, magic is a pure and positive art form. It's meant to *help* and *heal* those in need and can only come from those with goodness in their hearts."

The king sank back into his chair and held his head, dizzy with confusion.

"Oh dear, I've overwhelmed you," Madame Weatherberry said. "Let me simplify it for you, then. *Magic is good, magic is good, magic is good. Witchcraft is bad, witchcraft is bad, witchcraft is—*"

"Don't patronize me, woman—I heard you!" the king griped. "Give me a moment to wrap my head around it!"

Champion let out a long sigh and massaged his temples. It was usually difficult for him to process information so shortly after a nap, but this was an entirely different beast. The king covered his eyes and concentrated, as if he were reading a book behind his eyelids.

"You're saying magic is not the same as witch-craft?"

"Correct," Madame Weatherberry said with an encouraging nod. "Apples and oranges."

"And the two are different in nature?"

"Polar opposites, sir."

"So, if not *witches*, what do you call people who practice magic?"

Madame Weatherberry held her head high with pride. "We call ourselves *fairies*, sir."

"*Fairies?*" the king asked.

"Yes, *fairies*," she repeated. "Now do you under-stand my desire to enlighten your perspective? The world's concern isn't with fairies who practice magic, it's with witches who commit witchcraft. But tragi-cally, we've been grouped together and condemned as one and the same for centuries. Fortunately, with my guidance and your influence, we are more than capable of rectifying this."

"I'm afraid I disagree," the king said.

"I beg your pardon?" Madame Weatherberry replied.

"One man may steal because of greed, and another may steal for survival, but they're both thieves—it doesn't matter if one has *goodness* in his heart."

"But, sir, I thought I made it perfectly clear that witchcraft is the crime, not magic."

"Yes, but *both* have been considered sinful since the beginning of time," Champion went on. "Do you know how difficult it is to redefine something for society? It took me *decades* to convince my kingdom that potatoes aren't poisonous—and people still avoid them in the markets!"

Madame Weatherberry shook her head in disbelief. "Are you comparing an innocent race of people to potatoes, sir?"

"I understand your objective, Madame, but the world isn't ready for it—heck, *I'm* not ready for it!

If you want to save the fairies from unfair punishment, then I suggest you teach them to keep quiet and resist the urge to use magic! That would be far easier than convincing a stubborn world to change its ways."

"Resist the *urge*? Sir, you can't be serious!"

"Why not? Normal people live above temptation every day."

"Because you're implying magic comes with an off switch—like it's some sort of *choice*."

"Of course magic is a choice!"

"NO! IT! IS! NOOOOT!"

For the first time since their interaction had begun, Madame Weatherberry's pleasant temperament changed. A shard of deep-seated anger pierced through her cheery disposition and her face fell into a stony, intimidating glare. It was as if Champion were facing a different woman altogether—a woman who should be feared.

"Magic is *not* a choice," Madame Weatherberry said sharply. "*Ignorance* is a choice. *Hatred* is a choice. *Violence* is a choice. But someone's *existence* is never a choice, or a fault, and it's certainly not a crime. You would be wise to educate yourself."

Champion was too afraid to say another word. It may have been his imagination, but the king could have sworn the storm outside was intensifying as Madame Weatherberry's temper rose. It was obviously a state she rarely surrendered to because her apprentices seemed as uneasy as the king. The fairy closed her eyes, took a deep breath, and calmed herself before continuing their discussion.

"Perhaps we should give His Majesty a demonstration," Madame Weatherberry suggested. "Tangerina? Skylene? Will you please show King Champion why magic isn't a choice?"

Andrew Scott

Chris Colfer is a #1 *New York Times* bestselling author and Golden Globe–winning actor. He was honored as a member of the TIME 100, *Time* magazine's annual list of the one hundred most influential people in the world, and his books include *Struck By Lightning: The Carson Phillips Journal*; *Stranger Than Fanfiction*; the Land of Stories series: *The Wishing Spell*, *The Enchantress Returns*, *A Grimm Warning*, *Beyond the Kingdoms*, *An Author's Odyssey*, and *Worlds Collide*; and *A Tale of Magic*. . . .